THE FIDDLE
IS
THE
DEVIL'S INSTRUMENT
And Other Forbidden Knowledge

13 Tales of Lovecraftian Horror

By
Brett J. Talley

JournalStone

JOURNALSTONE
YOUR LINK TO ARTISTIC TALENT

JournalStone books may be ordered through booksellers or by contacting:

JournalStone
www.journalstone.com

The views expressed in this work are solely those of the authors and do not necessarily reflect the views of the publisher, and the publisher hereby disclaims any responsibility for them.

ISBN: 978-1-945373-63-3   (sc)
ISBN: 978-1-945373-64-0   (ebook)
ISBN: 978-1-945373-65-7   (hc)

JournalStone rev. date: April 21, 2017

Library of Congress Control Number: 2017934034

Printed in the United States of America

Cover Art – photo images & Design: Miai313 – 99designs
David Revoy wikimedia.org/wiki/File:Environments-21-cave.png
Borja Pindado - wikimedia.org/wiki/File:Rhan-Tegoth_by_Borja_Pindado.jpg
Emma Wright - deviantart.com/art/3D-Tentacles-192522336
Shutterstock - artist-young-elegant-man-emotional-185025365

Edited by: Aaron J. French

For Annie

Table of Contents

The Transcriptionist's Accomplice:

An Introduction
By
Ronald Malfi

A few years ago, in a hotel in the mountains of Utah, a character of suspicious design emptied his fourth and final Scotch and soda at the hotel bar, then ratcheted up from the barstool and teetered momentarily before groping for the book on the bar top that he'd brought with him that evening. This character had planned to smoke a cigar in the courtyard by the hotel fire pit, but freezing temperatures and a willowy snowfall had changed his plans. He'd spent the past two hours at the bar, engrossed in the book, and ignoring the assembly-line of patrons who had come and gone throughout the night.

As he stepped away from the bar now, a woman seated two barstools down from him chanced a last-second conversation: "What *is* that book you've been reading all night?"

Our reluctant hero came to a halt upon the scuffed tiles of the barroom floor, and wavered there, albeit for just a second or two, like a fork stuck with its tines in the earth. He turned and looked at the woman. She was maybe in her late forties, with a pretty face framed in waves of sterling hair, and big thighs straining within a pair of black Lycra pants.

Our hero glanced at the book, and at the hulking, tentacle-faced beastie on the cover, then said to the woman: "It's called *That Which Should Not Be*. It's my autobiography."

"You're auto—"

"Joking." He handed her the book. "It's a Lovecraft-inspired novel."

She examined the cover art, glanced at the back, then thumbed through the pages. "Is it like Stephen King?"

Jesus Christ, help me, thought our hero.

"No," he said. "Not really. You've never heard of H.P. Lovecraft?"

"No," the woman said, handing our hero back the book. "Sounds like a romance writer."

Jesus, poke my eardrums out, thought our hero.

"I suppose," he said, because the Scotch was making him more pliant than usual.

The woman took an iPhone about the size of a small television set from her purse, and began clacking her polished nails against the screen. "I'm writing it down so I can pick it up later. Sounds intriguing. What was the author's name again?"

"Talley," said our hero. "Brett J. Talley."

"Okay, great." The woman smiled. "I'm going to read this book and see what it's all about."

"God save the queen," remarked our hero. Then he bid the woman farewell and hunted out, in his quasi-inebriated state, the rank of elevators that would carry him to his fifth-floor hotel room.

Our hero—and by now, you may have an idea who this particular hero is—returned to his room, instantly stripped off all his clothes, then arrived in the bathroom where he shut the door, cranked the hot water in the tub, then sat cross-legged on the bathroom floor to read while the atmosphere slowly resolved itself into a sauna.

Our hero—me, in other words—finished the book thirty minutes later. By that time, the bathroom mirror was fogged up and sweat was spilling in rivulets down my face. (My fingers had dampened the final few pages of the novel, like some strange watermark that was somehow fitting for those pages.) What I had surmised when I first started reading the novel was confirmed after finishing it—I was carried along as an almost-character in this tale (or tales, as it were) that was horrifying and bleak but also somehow comforting and familiar. Two days earlier, when I opened the book and read the first page, I felt myself settling down as if in an old worn and familiar chair, lulled into security just from those first few sentences. I knew where we were going and I was anxious to get on the road.

Here's the thing: I'm not a huge fan of Lovecraft. I've always had a tough time picturing the *place* of his stories; his prose is often so mired in specific details that he has, for me, failed to set the stage, so to speak. However, I *do* enjoy other writers' takes on Lovecraft's mythos. Many times, these writers do a better job than the master himself, their prose more palatable to me than old Howard Phillips's. You want an analogy? This is sort of the same way I feel about the Beatles. The Beatles were unparalleled songwriters, but I find that pretty much every cover version of their songs by other artists is better. Joe Cocker belting "With a Little Help From My Friends," anyone? Ray Charles's haunting rendition of "Let It Be"? C'mon, people...

With Brett Talley's *That Which Should Not Be*, I finally found the quintessential Lovecraft translator, a Joe Cocker who could show me the emotion behind the chord progression. Soon after reading this book, Talley was considerate enough to publish a follow-up, *He Who Walks in Shadow*. Goddamn, I was hooked.

Fast-forward to just a few weeks ago, and the kind Mr. Talley had contacted our hero about the possibility of providing commentary on his forthcoming collection, *The Fiddle is the Devil's Instrument*, of which, if you're reading this introduction, you've already displayed the good sense to pick up a copy. For our hero, this was like Omaha Steaks calling up and asking if I'd eat a crate of prime rib if it happened to show up on my doorstep.

Needless to say, our hero, undaunted, accepted his assignment. Upon finishing the collection, he—I—shot off a tidy little blurb to our one Mr. Talley which goes as follows:

"It'll take less than a single page before you are fully enveloped into a world of dusty texts, Gothic séances, and old-world terrors. Brett J. Talley's latest sojourn   into the world of Lovecraftian horrors is like tasting a dark and mystic wine—one   which may or may not be laced with arsenic. This collection solidifies my adoration of Talley's work."

No sooner did our hero send this message did he receive a reply from the kind Mr. Talley, who, despite his etiquette, was justifiably motivated to ensure that our hero, whose penchant for not following directions has been evidenced time and time again, was able to read between the subtle lines and to arrive at something which, for all intents and purposes, basically said:

"Hey, dummy, I didn't ask for a blurb. I asked for an introduction. So if you could   kindly focus just a little bit more on the request at hand, that would be much appreciated, you dim-witted turd."

Or something to that effect.

So here I sit, opting instead for a steaming cup of strong Sumatran coffee instead of the company of one of the Beam brothers, hammering out this introduction for a collection that, in all honesty, needs no introduction. Talley's prose is assured, and dripping with atmosphere. From the opening of the titular story, as we are timewarped back to the middle of last century and guided through the creaking doors of Haven's Crest, to the "dangerous business" of the finale, the fetid breath of the wendigo like a tropical breeze against your flesh, you will be held...not as a prisoner, but that of an accomplice of sorts. Because that's what it's like reading this book—you are somehow an accomplice in all that transpires. A co-conspirator. Open your eyes and the year is 1715, and those arcane walls of Miskatonic rise up out of the fog. Blink again and the dry wind is blowing...and then the animals vanish...and then it's worse. And if you've read *That Which Should Not Be,* you'll traverse these tales with some old friends. (As I began "The Return of the Witch Queen," the good Carter Weston materialized out of the gloom, propped an elbow against my armchair, and, his eyes alive in the firelight coming from my hearth, proclaimed, "My, but I hope this plays out well for us, old friend." I said I hoped it did as well.)

Set a fire in the fireplace, pour yourself some blood-red wine, settle into your favorite chair, and listen to the book cover creak as you open this mystic tome.

"This Mr. Talley," says Carter Weston, leaning over our hero's shoulder as he stares down at the book you are now holding in your hands. "He is...how shall I say? Less a writer of fiction and more like a transcriptionist. Do you understand?"

"I do."

"And he's got more tales yet to tell," says Carter Weston.

"That's right," says our hero.

Shall we begin?

—Ronald Malfi
February 18, 2017
Annapolis, Maryland

THE FIDDLE
IS
THE
DEVIL'S INSTRUMENT

The Fiddle is the Devil's Instrument

When Cannon Danvers called me to one of his famous séances, my first inclination was to decline. Others would have given their right arm or other critical body part to receive such an invitation. Cannon Danvers was a name whispered from the shrouded cities of the Far East to the still-smoldering capitals of Europe to the hills of Kentucky, where I claim ancestry. He was the man who, in the earliest flower of his youth, finally convinced Houdini of the power of mysticism. He had predicted both World Wars and had, in the darkest days of the latest conflict, assured President Roosevelt in a private meeting that we would come through—even if, like Moses of old, the president would not live to see it.

And he just so happened to be my uncle, my mother's older brother and a stain on the family name. My mother had been a pure-hearted, God-fearing woman, and if she knew her boy was going to be sitting at a table with a known devil-worshiper—and while he attempted to communicate with the spirits at that—well, I guess she'd drop dead right there. But she'd passed the spring before, a week after we celebrated V-E day, and I'm thankful that the gift of peace allowed me to make it home on leave from France to be with her in those final moments. But my point being, she was gone now to the Jesus whom she trusted and loved, and nothing could trouble her. As for me, I'd seen enough of war and death to have lost more than a little faith in God. So ironically, I figured a little proof of the devil would be good for my soul.

I'd never met Cannon Danvers. I wondered if his invitation was some attempt to close old wounds, or maybe even to reward me for my service to my country. Whatever was the case, I returned the RSVP with an affirmative and spent a significant portion of my combat pay on a new dinner jacket.

The night came, April 30, the May-eve, which some folks call the Beltane. I knew a little bit about it, about the fires the ancients built to chase away the evil spirits that were said to gather on that evening. I'd read about that—and a lot of other things some folks might frown upon. I guess I have a little bit of my uncle in me after all.

Still, I'd never gone so far as to partake in any of the forbidden rites or celebrations of pagan festivals about which I'd read. I'd never been ready to make that leap of dark faith. Then came the invitation.

Cannon lived on a plantation east of Georgetown, Kentucky, called Haven's Crest, the home of the Danvers line since Temperance Danvers brought his branch of the family down from Massachusetts following the War of Independence. It passed to Cannon, he being the eldest son, when my grandfather died—well before Cannon began his career as a spiritualist. I suspected my mother resented him as much for the inheritance that had been denied her as for his ungodly ways. And I wondered sometimes if she resented me a little bit, too. For while it might have been the case that my grandfather saw fit to bypass her because she was a woman, it was just as likely that he had frowned upon the fact that she had a child out of wedlock with a man who was a mystery. Truth is, I don't even know my father's name. Though Mother might have died godly, everyone makes mistakes.

I arrived at Haven's Crest an hour after sundown, as instructed, driving the 1937 Model T that had belonged to my mother prior to her death. An attendant directed me to a parking spot next to a line of newer, finer models, and it struck me that I would probably feel more comfortable amongst the staff than the other guests at this party. I parked and fell in line behind an older couple who had also just arrived. I followed them up the path, lit by torches that ran to the front of the house. Music wafted down, beckoning us onward.

That night I entered the ancestral home of my family for the first time—and I did so as a guest. It struck me as ironic, how the accident of birth can change things; how, if I'd been born a generation before in the place of my uncle, such an estate would be mine. Instead, I had little but a shack and forty acres to my name. I'd pondered it often during the war, as I fought and killed men who I might have been, had the spin of the wheel gone differently.

The house was as elegant within as without. A great staircase hugged the wall, twisting down to the grand foyer where I stood. No doubt it had made for dramatic entrances by southern belles in an age dead and gone if not yet forgotten. The house evidently had electricity; it would have been passing strange for it not to. But our gracious host had chosen to light it this night with tall, black candles. There were hundreds of them, and though the comingling of their illumination provided enough visibility, a hazy smoke hung in the air. The flickering flames danced within it, and the shadows they cast seemed to have deeper forms and more substance than they should have.

I moved cautiously from the entrance to the parlor, my palms sweating. Guests milled about, chatting, laughing, though their friendliness seemed forced to me, as it always did in these settings. I did not care for the wealthy. Or, I should say, I did not care to be amongst them, particularly in large groups. I did not belong. I knew it. They knew it. What's the point in fighting it? I filled a cup with punch from a bowl made of carved crystal and set out to explore the house.

My feet carried me to where the voices died, away from the crowd, into the depths of the home. I walked down a hall that ended in two polished wooden doors. One was cracked open, and flickering light spilled into the hallway. I opened it, and stepped into a mighty library. It was the kind you'd see in the films, with shelves that went all the way to the ceiling and a ladder that moved on a track from one corner of the room to the next. And books, so many books, too many to arrange neatly, so they were stacked upon one another in several places. And in the center of the room, reading by the light of an electric lamp, sat a man who could only be Cannon Danvers.

"Mr. Danvers," I said, feeling foolish to have interrupted him, even more foolish to refer to him by my own last name. He looked up at me, studied me for an instant before his face softened and he broke into a smile.

"Why, my good fellow, I believe I could certainly call you the same. You must be my sister's boy."

"Yes, sir," I said, standing straighter as he rose from his chair, as if he were an old drill sergeant checking to see if my boots were spit-shined. I'd known natural leaders before, the good and the bad; certain men can command a room merely by their presence. Patton was that kind of man. So was Cannon Danvers. As he strode across the room, I knew he was someone other men would follow. He was not at all what I expected from a spiritualist and a medium.

"So you are Amelia's son," he said, shaking my hand. "I was sorry to hear of her passing. And I was sorrier still that we were never able to mend the...break that separated us." His eyes fell to his feet, as if the shame of it was truly more than he could bear. My questions about the impetus for my invitation were answered. Cannon Danvers wanted to make amends with my dead mother through me.

"I know she always loved you, sir," I said, and I thought there was at least a good chance it was true. Blood, after all, cleanses all manner of sins.

"Perhaps, perhaps. She'd probably kill me, and maybe you too, if she knew you were here tonight. But I'm glad you came."

"Well, sir, I love my mother, but it's hard to come back from war and remain prudish about such matters. I figure God let me get through it so I could see everything there is to see, even if some of those things are forbidden."

The corner of his mouth crept up into a smile. "Yes, I like that view. I like it very much. It is one I have always followed myself. Come over here," he said, beckoning to me before turning and walking back to his desk. I followed.

A book lay open on the table, its pages yellowed, cracked. Cannon tapped the lamp with a finger.

"Special light bulb," he said. "It won't damage the paper in the book, even when it's as old as this one. The candles outside are for show, of course. Atmosphere. But in here, we don't take chances with such things. Do you know what this is?"

I did not, of course, but I hesitated to be so bold in my ignorance.

"It's nothing to be ashamed of, my boy. There are few who would. It is a Latin translation of an ancient work, the Egyptian Book of the Dead."

From somewhere deep within the house came the shrill sound of a bow drawn across a fiddle.

"Pyramid funerary text?"

A fire leapt into my uncle's eyes, and he flashed a toothy grin. I felt a surge of pride in myself. This had pleased him.

"Very good. You know your ancient faiths. But no, this is something different, something most scholars have never imagined, much less seen. This is the *true* Book of the Dead. Not a text on how to send man into the afterlife. No, this is the book that can bring him back."

The distant fiddle sounded again, tingling a high-pitched squeal as the player sawed heavily with his bow.

"Bring them back," I said, shivering. "Why would you want to do that?"

"Oh, many reasons, my boy. Many reasons. To reveal secrets lost. To impart mysteries undreamt of. Or, as the case may be, to simply show that I can." Someone hollered in the rooms beyond, and the band kicked off a reel. Cannon glanced toward the door. "So the party begins. Shall we join them?"

"What about the book?"

He grinned. "The book is for later"

He led me back through the maze of corridors, into the grand hall that must have dominated the house. For it was massive, spanning the length of the structure, with great high ceilings that sparkled like the heavens. A stage had been erected at one end, and upon it a band played bluegrass. A man fiddled like the devil, and the caller sang out a song I had never heard about nine yards of other cloth.

"I'll leave you now," said Cannon. "But don't worry. I'll find you again. Make yourself at home."

With that he seemed to glide into the crowd, vanishing into a throng of his gala-clad guests.

"He's something, isn't he?"

I turned to find a woman, dressed in a long, black gown, wearing a mask to match it, adorned in feathers the color of ravens.

"Why, yes, yes he is."

The woman smiled, her lips parting to reveal perfectly straight teeth.

"You've never been here before, have you?"

"This would be my first visit."

"Come on," she said, taking my hand. "Let me get you a drink."

I followed her to a bar that had been erected on the far side. A waiter chipped away ice from a massive block into a glass, drowning it in generous pours of bourbon. It was my kind of party.

"So how do you know Cannon?" The band fired up a Virginia reel, and even the well-heeled Louisville and Lexington types showed their country blood.

"We're related, actually. He's my uncle."

"Ah," she said, "so you are the famous nephew. Cannon speaks highly of you."

"Well that's flattering, ma'am, though I can't say what he would know about me."

"Oh, Cannon knows a great many things, more than any normal man. You should understand that."

"I'm coming to. So how do you know my uncle?"

"We were lovers once. Oh don't look so scandalized. I'm a grown woman, and I can do as I like." She took a step toward me, reached up and rubbed the collar of my jacket between her thumb and her forefinger. The sound of the band had died away as quickly as it had roared to life; now only the fiddler played, sawing a lonesome song of love lost. She leaned forward, her lips touching the small hairs on my ear. "But I'm all on my own, now. And so very lonely. Look for me, when the end is near, if you need a guide to find your way."

The crowd surged forward, and she receded into it, swept away from me like a pebble on the beach. I had no time to think on it for Cannon Danvers had taken the stage.

The room dimmed as servants extinguished all but a handful of candles. The members of the band vanished into the growing darkness. All save one—the fiddler, who stood behind Cannon, bow set at the ready.

"My friends, thank you all for joining me on this very special evening. Many of you have come before. Some of you have seen extraordinary things. But I assure you, nothing can prepare you for what you will witness tonight."

A murmur spread through the crowd, excitement and fear, not unlike what I had once heard on the battlefields of Europe.

"I am no maker of tricks or conjurer of illusions. I see things other men cannot see. I know things other men cannot know. In the last few years we have come to understand the essence of matter itself. We have harnessed the power of the atom. For good...and for destruction. But there is knowledge far older, and far more powerful, knowledge that can be found in this book."

He held up an ancient tome, and even in the dim light I could see that it was the Egyptian *Book of the Dead* he had shown me in the library before. The fiddler, who until then had stood still and silent, now drug his bow across the strings of his instrument, playing a harsh and evil note that rung just barely within the range of human hearing. The atmosphere thickened, and I grinned. My uncle was quite the showman.

"Yes, I have powers undreamt of by the common magician, and unimagined even by mighty Solomon himself, the lord king of all the mystics. But for the magic we will do tonight, I will need your help. All of your help." The fiddler's note quivered. "When I speak the words of power, each line requires an answer. That answer, you will give. Say it simply. Say it loud. Iä! Iä! Say it!"

The crowd answered back: "Iä! Iä!" But I stayed silent. I had read in my studies that while a Christian man could fear no evil if he happened to find himself in the midst of a black mass—however such a predicament might come to pass—he who took part in the ceremony, even if in jest, bound himself to the coven. He had become a member of it, as sure as if he'd pledged his fealty to it, or signed the Black Book in his own blood. Superstition, perhaps, but I was not about to cross it.

I felt eyes on me, and I wondered if maybe someone had noticed my reticence, someone who might report me to my uncle. I looked about, and my gaze locked on hers—the woman whom I had met earlier was staring at me, her dark eyes shining behind her mask. I thought she was grinning, but then a figure passed between us and when he was gone, so was she.

"Very good. Very good," said my uncle. "The power is strong tonight, and I do believe that we will find profitable magic this Beltane. You will notice that no fires burn in my fields this evening. No, we have not lit the bane, nor shall we. For we do not seek to chase away the spirits, but to welcome them."

The assemblage laughed and clapped and cheered. I glanced above and noticed that the few remaining candles cast eerie shadows on the ceiling. Undulating black globes that stared down upon us like great, empty eyes. On the stage, my uncle had placed the book on the stand before him. He flipped pages, staring down intently as he went, searching. Then he smiled wide, having apparently found the spell he was looking for. Behind him, the fiddler played so softly that you couldn't quite hear him. Not with your ears at least. Only with your soul.

"And now we begin, my friends. Now we open the way. Now we call to those beyond. Now we shall see the forbidden."

He held up his hands, shoulder length apart, palms facing us. Even from that distance, I could see him close his eyes.

"From the realm of the living to the realm of the dead, we beseech thee. *Iä! Iä!*"

The crowd answered as one.

"Anubis, open the gate. Khephri, purify our hearts. Ma'at, find us worthy. Thoth, record our prayer. *Iä! Iä!*"

The crowd answered again, louder.

"Come, Osiris! Come, Sekhmet! Come, Sobek and Heket! *Iä! Iä!*"

As the crowd chanted in reply, even louder than before, I felt a hand slip into mine. "You don't want to be here when he finishes," she whispered into my ear, as the discordant sound of the fiddle rippled up my spine.

"Why not?" I turned and looked at her, her eyes grabbing me no less forcefully than if she had clasped her hand upon my shoulder.

"You know why. You know what's coming."

"But I don't," I said. But as the words left my lips, I knew it was a lie. I did know, somehow. Even if it was only deep down, somewhere that I couldn't quite see or understand. She smiled, and I let her pull me away, all the way to the door to the great hall. No one barred our way, no one stopped us. Not until she stopped, just beyond the threshold.

"You cannot stay," she said. "But you must see."

I looked back into the room. I squinted, and then rubbed my eyes. For something was wrong. The air shimmered. I felt as though I was looking through glass into a world that had sunk beneath the sea. The image was distorted. The people in the crowd seemed to sway, to extend beyond themselves, grotesquely and unnaturally. Only the stage was clear. Only my uncle, and the fiddler who played behind him.

"Make way for Hastur. Make way for He Who Walks in Shadow. Make way for the Crawling Chaos. Come forth, Nyarlathotep! *Iä! Iä!*"

There was a crack, sharp and sickening, like the breaking of many bones all at once. The crowd shrieked in unison, but they did not run. A shadow fell upon them, and then, as they screamed, they began to dance. Legs and arms jerked, spasmed, as if they did not fully control them. Or perhaps it was that their new masters were unfamiliar with such appendages. My uncle's manic smile faded, and fear crept into the crevices of his face. Only one man seemed unfazed, the one who played a tune I thanked God above I could no longer hear. But he had changed, too, for he was no longer a man. No man's skin can turn as black as the abyss. No man's eyes can burn with a fire that would devour souls. No man *smiles* like that. And no man *plays* like that.

The candles flared, and the dancers turned to torches, skin melting off bones. And yet still they cried out. Still, they danced.

I saw the moment my uncle's mind broke, as he gibbered and cackled on the stage, as he tore at his own eyes lest he see what he had done. And the last thing I saw, before the woman, my savior, pulled me mercifully away, was that *man*, that beast, still fiddling.

We ran. Out of the house. Down the hill. As the mansion burst into flames and turned night into day. We didn't stop until we reached the road.

"You knew," I said, as I doubled over with my hands on my knees. "You knew and you didn't do anything to stop it."

She stood there, as elegant as if we still danced in the grand ballroom that now burned with Satan's fire. "I didn't come to stop it," she said.

"Then why are you here?"

She took a step forward, extended one lithe hand and lifted my chin with a single finger. An orange light flashed in her eyes, and it wasn't from the flames. "I came for you. Cannon Danvers, his steps always led here, to this night, to this place. But you, Cyrus, you have many steps left to take. And what a journey it will be."

There was the sound of rending fabric. Her dress fell away, and two great, black raven wings spread wide from behind her. With one mighty sweep they lifted her into the sky. The firelight flashed across her body as she blotted out the moon, and I let blessed unconsciousness take me into its waiting arms.

The Apotheosis of a Rodeo Clown

The biker they called Tonto was already helping Hog drag the girl down into the mine by the time I decided what I needed to do. Tonto means stupid in Spanish. I can't say much else about the Sons of Dagon, especially much of anything positive, but they had a way with names.

As I looked down at my fake stump hand, covered in fake stump blood, I made the decision to save the girl. That was the clown code, after all.

But I probably better back up and start at the beginning.

I'm not like most other people. I'm a full-time rodeo clown. A real professional. Not one of these kids looking to score a few bucks when the show rolls through town on the weekend. Been doing it the better part of my adult life. Hell, I clowned with Mr. Flint Rasmussen himself, and that still means something in certain parts of the country.

Clowning wasn't always my dream. When I was a kid, I wanted to be a bull rider. I was going to be the one to finally score the Perfect Ten. Had some talent for it, too. Started out with calves, like most of the young 'uns. Then when I was fourteen years old, I rode my first bull, a charbray by the name of Bodacious.

Now Bodacious was one clever son-of-a-bitch. He had this trick he'd pull where he'd throw his legs up in the air in such a way that threw you forward. Then he'd jerk his head back and smash you in the face. Weren't too many that rode Bodacious who didn't have a broken nose to show for it.

They warned me about that when I got on him. I told myself, "He ain't going to get me in the face." And by God, he didn't. Course, when he bucked forward and I pulled back instead of letting my body weight go with him, I completely lost control. He threw me alright, and landed a back kick right in my spine, like something from a Saturday-morning cartoon. I didn't break my nose, but I did break my spine.

Nothing too serious, as back breaks go. I'm not a paraplegic or anything. But they did tell me no more bull riding. And that was that. The end of a dream. So I decided I'd do the next best thing. If I couldn't ride the bull, I'd fight the bull.

That's the rodeo clowns true name—a bullfighter. Yeah, we wear the face paint and the silly pants and a shirt that would look good in a San Francisco gay pride parade, but we are warriors at heart. And like all good warriors, we have a code. And rule number one of the Rodeo Clown Code is that you never leave an innocent in harm's way. Not when you can step in front of whatever's coming for them.

Which brings me to the girl.

We'd been doing a show in Lone Pine, a little town in California's Owen Valley, resting in a dale between the Alabama Hills. Sounds picturesque, but it was a parched town in a dry desert where water never flowed, except through the aqueducts that headed south to Los Angeles so the city could drink up Lone Pine's future, present, and past.

Most of the guys hated shows like that, in little places soon forgotten. They dreamed of the big time in Amarillo or Tulsa or Cheyenne. But not me. People in little towns like that, they ain't got nothing. So when we come, we are the world to them. For a few precious hours, we can bring them joy. Real joy. Yeah, the Lone Pine fairground was broke down, the termites had eat up the wood of the fence, and the sign didn't even light up anymore, but it was magical to me. So I didn't even notice the guys in leather cuts with "Sons of Dagon" sown in great, red letters across the back, hanging around the gates.

We did our thing. Danced our dance with the bulls. Nobody got hurt and the crowd, small though it was, enjoyed it and roared their approval. A good evening's work, with not much to do after but get drunk and think about the next night's show.

"Yo, clown!"

I didn't hesitate to look up, as if the guy was actually calling my name. Dude was big, but not fat. Thick around the chest and the middle, bald head but full beard. Basically he looked like he'd stepped off the set of *Sons of Anarchy*. Hell, maybe he had.

"Got a proposition for you." He spit a line of tobacco juice into the dust. "You interested in a little side work?"

"Depends," I said. "What you got?"

Two other men in the same leather cut-off jackets appeared beside him. One of them was tall, skinny, and shook like an alcoholic after a bender when the money runs out. I would learn later that he was called Tonto. Never learned his real name. Never learned any of their real names. I'm not sure even *they* remembered them. The other guy was as chubby as Tonto was skinny, a big ol' boy who didn't seem like he'd be all that comfortable on the back of a motorcycle. The hog is supposed to be the bike. And, in fact, that was his name. Hog. I'd learn all that later, of course. For now, they didn't talk. Just the one in the middle did that.

"Rodeo. Small, private event. Couple hundred in it for you and for anybody else you get."

He grinned. Something about it I definitely didn't like. I'd say I should have listened to my instincts, but fact is, I needed the money. Professional rodeo clowns aren't exactly highly paid, and the benefits are for shit.

"Alright," I said. "I'm in."

"Think you can get a few of the boys to come along?"

"Sure thing. As many as you need."

"Not too many. Just a couple. And another thing, this is sorta a Halloween-type event. So you think you can bloody it up a bit?"

It was June. Strange, but people had asked for stranger.

"Sure."

"Hell yeah," he said, slapping me on the back. "We'll pick you up tomorrow. This time. Right here."

The three men turned and walked off into the gathering dark, the thin one cackling all the way to the parking lot.

It wasn't hard to find volunteers. Two hundred bucks for a night's work was unheard of. Sure, there was probably something else too it, but when the money's good, who gives a rip?

They returned the next night, just as they had promised, as our last show was coming to a close. They pulled up in a van; the muscular one was driving.

"No bikes?"

He scowled at me, and the look made me wonder if he'd ever killed a man. "What," he said, "you wanna ride bitch?"

I laughed. He did not. "Guess not," I said. "What's your name, anyway?"

"Piston. And that's all you need to know. Get in the back."

"Hey!" Tonto stuck his head out the window. "You're supposed to be dressed up for Halloween."

I held up a plastic bag. "We'll change in the back."

He grunted, which I took as a sign of approval. I climbed in the back of the van, and two of my buddies followed. They were young guys, not locals exactly but Californians who worked the season when the tour came through.

There were no seats other than the two in the front, so we made ourselves as comfortable as possible and hoped that Piston was a more conscientious driver than might be expected. Hog was passed out in the bed of the van, fortunately out of our way.

I emptied the contents of the bag on the floor—mostly fake blood and cheap bandages—and passed them around to Sam and Jake, the other two clowns that had joined me. I call them clowns, but they were of the new set that eschewed the classic getup in favor of a traditional cowboy look, so I was the only one wearing paint. I'd gone with the more John Wayne Gacy approach—white face, blue triangles over my eyes, red mouth painted to points. That's the thing about Gacy; any clown could have told you he was a bad dude. Real clowns outline their paint in nice, gentle curves. It's less aggressive, sends the signal that no, we are not actually going to kill you. Points are aggressive. Sharp angles, frightening. Should have known Gacy was a killer. He wore it right there on his face.

Tonto leaned over the back of his seat and gawked at us. He watched us squirt fake blood and black paint into our hands and spread it across our clothes, our arms, our faces.

"Whatcha doin?" Tonto said.

"You wanted Halloween, right? We're zombies."

Tonto giggled stupidly. "Zombie clowns." He giggled some more. "Whatdaya think about that, Piston? They're clown zombies."

Piston didn't answer. He seemed to be a man of few words. Tonto turned back around, but every now and then I'd hear him giggle to himself again.

The only windows in the van were in the back, so I leaned against the wheel-well and watched the place we'd just been slip into the past. The Alabama Hills rose around me, named by southern sympathizers for the mighty warship that was the pride of the Confederacy. I wondered about those people, southerners who'd come west in '49 looking for their fortunes. By definition, then, they didn't own slaves, couldn't legally in the territory they were headed, even if they could have afforded them. Like so many their loyalty was to the southern earth, the states that had given them birth, the rivers that divided them. I wondered how they felt when the Alabama was sunk off the coast of France. Not everyone was disappointed. Just beyond the Alabama Hills lay the Kearsarge range, named after the ship that sent her to the bottom of the sea. What a country.

"So where are we going?" I asked.

"Mining town," said Piston. "Up in the mountains."

"You guys go up there a lot?"

"Yeah. We go up there a lot."

"Do people still live there?"

"Nope. Abandoned."

That wasn't a surprise. The Alabama Hills had once drawn men with little money and big dreams from every part of the country and even the world. Only one in a hundred made it. Ten times that ended up dead, while the rest were just broken. Then the big conglomerates came through and bought up the hills. That's when the mines went deep and towns sprung up around them. I call them towns, but they were little more than camps for the men—a saloon, dry goods store, maybe a brothel if they were lucky.

"This town got a name?" Piston caught my eye in the rearview. I couldn't see his mouth, but I knew he was smiling.

"Sure it does. They called it Sutter's End."

Sutter's End. So that was it. I began to wonder if I'd made a mistake. Easy money always comes with a price, and the old saw about something that seems too good to be true is more often than not on target.

Sutter's End had a nasty reputation. The mine had closed some fifty years before, and the town had died with it. The story that everyone knew was that the main shafts were running dry, but the bosses wanted to squeeze a few more million out of the hole. So they ordered the men to blast a new shaft down from the main one. Of course blasting when you were that deep already was nothing short of taking your life in your own hands, but back in those days that sort of thing went. Still does if we're being honest with each other. So when the charges detonated, down came the supports—and the walls and ceilings with them.

That was the official story at least. Tragedies like that always have another, one more shrouded in the twice-told and the unsupported. And Sutter's End had a doozy. The story, as the folks who lived at the bottom of the Alabama Hills told it, was that the charges worked just fine. Better than fine, even. That when they went off, they opened something more than just a new shaft. Nobody was ever quite so certain or so specific as to what exactly that something more was. But whatever came out of there took the miners. The people of the town, the ones who made it out alive, fled. Left everything behind and just went. So it stayed for years, till time dimmed the fear enough that enterprising grave robbers stripped the town bare. But even now, whispers would sometimes float down from Sutter's End, and no one dared to go up there at night to find out where they came from. No one, it seemed, but the Sons of Dagon.

And us.

The sun was setting by the time the town came into view. A thick cloud of dust rolled down the hill as we drove up, and when we pulled into what remained of the town, we saw why. It was chaos. When you've spent as much time clowning as I have, you've seen just about every type of man, and you learn quick not to judge them too much by what you see. But as I watched men bigger and meaner-looking than Piston spinning around the town square on giant bikes of shimmering chrome, metal bars shaped like bones, skulls with devil horns curving off of them between the handles, I was afraid. I glanced at Sam and Jake and saw the same look on their faces.

The van came to a stop. Piston threw open the rear doors and we hopped out. It was a party alright. There were bikers everywhere, sporting the leather cuts that read Sons of Dagon across the back, with some sort of emblem beneath it that I didn't recognize, like something out of one of those monster movies that comes on the television after midnight. I didn't like to look at it, so I didn't examine it for long. It was a face of sorts, one with evil eyes and what looked like tentacles that hung down where the mouth should be.

There wasn't much left of the town, and it didn't seem like there had been that much there to begin with. One central street with buildings on either side. At the end they'd erected a stage where a band was playing, heavy on the metal guitar with drums that sounded like thunder. The arena was set up off on the other end, and I recognized a cowboy leaning up against a cattle carrier next to it.

"Dan Travis," I said, walking up and taking his hand with the one I hadn't wrapped in bloody bandages.

"Well, I'll be damned," he said. "What the hell are you doing here?"

"Same thing as you, I guess."

"Part of this circus, too, huh?" He pulled out a pack of cigarettes and offered me one. I declined. "If I had it to do over, I might have passed." The rumble of a bike and a hollered obscenity punctuated the thought. He looked at me and squinted. "You supposed to be dead or something?"

"Something," I said. "When's this show getting started anyway?"

"They said we was waiting on you. So I guess any time now. Suits me just fine. I'd like to get the hell clear of here before it gets too dark."

I looked around at our surroundings. The town wasn't on a hill, precisely. More like a high canyon with low craggily walls on the sides. All and all, that meant the sun seemed to set faster than it should, and the darkness was more complete when it did.

"Yeah, I hear you. Any idea who's in charge?"

"That would be me."

I turned to see a man, older, but just as firmly built as Piston, standing behind me. He wore sunglasses, even though the day was long on gone, and his gray beard came to a point below his chin in a way that reminded me of the devil.

"I'm Goat," he said, offering his hand, and as I took it I thought that name worked with the beard too. "I run this show. Thank you boys for coming."

"Happy to be here," I lied. "Where'd you guys find this place?"

Goat snorted. "I own it. My granddaddy bought the land after the mine died. He needed a place for his family to have some privacy. As you can see, that family has grown." He swept the area with his hand, as if asking us to take it all in. And we did. About that time, the band fired up again.

"We take all kinds," he said, looking over his shoulder as the drummer hammered away. "Me, I prefer what you boys do. So that's why you're here. We'll get started in fifteen minutes. Be ready."

He started to walk off, but then he turned and pointed at my stump hand.

"Love the zombie get-up."

Fifteen minutes later, we were in the ring, ready to go. And I can tell you this, I've never been more afraid.

The band still played, but we were now the show, and most of the gang had made its way over to the makeshift corral. It was rotten wooden slates literally strung together with twine and bailing wire. A half-decent bull would have broke straight through and killed us all. But these bulls weren't half-decent. They were, in fact, the saddest I had ever seen, ten years past their prime if they were a day.

There were no riders, no real ones at least. The Sons of Dagon took turns. The crowd at the edge of the makeshift ring urged them on. Cursing, screaming, firing guns into the air. I doubted they had permits. I spent as much time dodging bottles as I did dodging bulls.

The energy in the air was foul and full of bloodlust. The crowd pulsated, seeming to squeeze in on us. Their shouts rose from a din to a roar till they seemed to cover all. They were pagan, visceral, somehow harkening back to a time of man's darkest age. One of the drunkest ones leapt the fence and ran toward a bull even as it struggled with its rider. The poor thing was terrified.

Over and over they rode them, till I was doubled over, hands on my knees, exhausted. But still, they rode.

It came to an end as suddenly as it had begun. Ten different guys had probably ridden that bull. The sweat was thick on its sides, its mouth foamed, and the sounds that came from its gullet no animal should make. Then it happened. The great beast gave one last massive thrust of its hind legs and then the rest of it tumbled over on its side. I knew then it was dead, probably dead before it hit the dirt. From somewhere deep below us, the earth rumbled.

The night sorta sputtered out then. The mood had changed. The Sons drifted away, one by one. The band stopped playing, packed up its kit, took down the stage, and was gone. It was full dark then, and the stars shone cold light upon us. Goat walked up, oddly somber. He handed each man a hundred dollars more than we were promised.

"You done good," he said, glancing down at my stump hand. "Night went sour. Sorry about that." He took a drag from his cigarette and coughed. "Piston and the boys'll take you back. But they got clean up duty tonight, so it might be a while. No idea what they'll do with that shit." He nodded at the dead bull. Flies had begun to gather. "Burn it, I guess." Then he too was gone.

Before long, it was just us. Sam and Jake leaned against the rotted fence, kicking at the dirt, silent and sullen. I didn't much feel like celebrating either, but there was no point in whining about it.

"I'm going to find Piston," I said.

They just ignored me, and I didn't bother trying to talk to them again. I headed out down what had been the main street. With the band and the bikes and the stage lights gone, it was dark in the way only the far wilderness can be dark, where not even the glow of distant city lights can ruin the night's completeness. In other words, it was dark as all hell, and even when my eyes adjusted, I could only barely make out the outlines of buildings. Add the unnatural quiet, and I admit to being somewhat unnerved. More than somewhat.

Laughter from one of the buildings. A beam of light and someone spilling out behind it into the street. I guess they saw me or heard me or something, because the next moment, the beam was shining in my direction. Then a giggle.

Tonto.

"Clown," he slurred, drunk or high or both. "Zombie clown. I like you."

A larger darkness stumbled out behind him—Piston. I expected Hog to follow. I did not expect him to be carrying someone else with him when he did. The two of them joined Tonto. I stopped dead in my tracks, suddenly quite aware of how bad things had just gotten for me. Tonto said something I couldn't hear. All three of them looked at me. A woman screamed. Hog slapped her hard across the face and told her to shut up. I almost thought I could see blood dripping from her nose.

"You coming, clown?" Piston slurred.

"Where you going?" I said, as natural as I could. I took a few steps toward them.

Piston raised an arm and pointed out down the road, to the rock face of the cliff that backed up to the town, at a patch of black night a little bit darker than the rest. It had been obscured by the stage before, but now it was clear. They started toward what could only be the opening of the mine, the one that had given birth to the town and then killed it. I said the first thing that came to my mind.

"Well fuck."

Every man—every woman too for that matter—has a moment where they have to decide who they are and who they will be. To decide whether to take a stand so they can stand themselves. This was my moment. The three men and one struggling woman disappeared into the darkness of the shaft. I knew what was next. They'd rape her, multiple times most likely. Then they'd kill her. And that would be it. No one would ever find the body, not down in that mine shaft. And just in case you think I was being all heroic, I also figured they'd kill me when they were done with her, the price of seeing something I wasn't supposed to see. So I made the only decision I could make. I followed them down into the mine.

I'm hadn't exactly formulated a plan, but one thing was immediately apparent—I couldn't see for shit. Fortunately, the three jackasses in front of me were as prepared as they were drunk, and I could follow the light of their bobbing flashlights. I stumbled after them, hoping to find a pickax or a shovel or just a damn big rock to use as a weapon. Otherwise, I wasn't sure what I was going to do when I caught up to them. When that actually happened—and without said pickax, shovel, or damn big rock—I basically made small talk.

"So," I said, in the hopes of announcing my presence without startling them and getting shot or stabbed, "what are we doing here, guys?"

Piston turned to me, and for the first time I saw the girl's face. She'd been crying, which was no surprise. But I wasn't prepared for the pain in those tear-filled eyes, or the look of absolute desperate hope that fell completely on me.

"You a believer?" Piston asked, in the strangest non sequitur of my life. Of all the things that had happened that night, it was his question that shocked me the most.

"Yeah," I said. "I guess so."

"You guess."

"Yeah."

"Well, we'll see if we can't make a believer out of you. And when you see what we got to show you, you won't need faith." He pointed to the wall of the mine. "You see that?"

And I did see it. A ragged opening, big enough for a man to enter through, but not comfortably. Obviously not a shaft running off the main or an opening made on purpose, either. If I had to guess, they'd been blasting when it broke through on its own. When something broke through. I thought back to the stories I had heard, about what had happened here, and I wondered just how much truth there was to the old local legends.

"Come on," Piston said. "We got something to show you."

"Yeah," Tonto said. "Something to show you." Then he laughed that big, stupid laugh as he disappeared behind Hog and the girl. Piston just kept on looking at me, and even through the gloom of the cave I could read his eyes. He was drunk, but he was sober enough to consider whether or not it was a good idea to have me along. Maybe he thought about killing me right then and there, I don't know. But he turned and slipped through the opening, and so did I.

Through the crack in the wall I saw something I could never have dreamed of, not in my wildest youth, not at my drunkest. This was no new mine shaft, no undiscovered cavern or cave. This was a room, a great, giant chamber with vaulted ceilings and massive columns. Something made by man. I hoped man had made it at least. I'd never seen the like. It put the great Temple of Karnak at Luxor to shame, made a mockery of the most extravagant constructions of the Greeks or the Romans.

The room glowed with some strange phosphorescence, illuminating a thick and unnatural mist that rolled and roiled along the ground. Suddenly the three drunken thugs didn't seem so fearsome, not nearly so as whatever lurked within this place, whatever or whoever had built it, and whatever had happened to those who had found it.

"Where are we?" I whispered into the darkness, as if there was anyone who could answer.

The trio and their captive stumbled down an arcade that lay between two great colonnades, and reluctantly, I followed. To flee into the darkened depths of the mine would have been more pleasant.

Tonto giggled. "This is neat. It's even better than I heard."

I felt a cold shiver arc down my spine. "You mean, you've never been here before?"

"Nah," he said. "Goat wouldn't let us. Only the higher…"

He surely would have said more, but Piston cut him off with a single look. Then he turned to me. "You ain't gotta stay if you're scared, clown."

"No," I said, "I'm good. Just wondering is all." He grunted at that, and we continued to walk.

I could see that at the end of the arcade was some sort of stone edifice. If this was a temple, I supposed it was an altar, though unlike anything I'd seen before. The stone work was exquisite, a swirl of rises and falls, of deep cuts and shallow valleys. Almost hurt to look at it, as if whatever image it produced made the eyes rebel. But whatever it was and whatever it signified, its creator possessed unmatched skill. I had worked as a stone mason in my youth, and I'd seen enough to know that this was the work of genius. Before it lay a stone slab, and beyond that a deep basin of similar construction. I realized then why the girl was here.

"So what are you guys planning to do?"

Piston turned to me.

"You said you wanted to see God."

I shook my head.

"I don't think I said that at all."

"Well, too bad." He jerked at Hog. "Get her ready."

Tonto started to cackle again, and the girl screamed. Stupidly, I made a grab at her. I'm not sure what I thought I'd do if I got a hold of her, and I never found out. Piston threw me away with a single flick of his caber-like arm. I fell to the ground and the cold mist enveloped me. I felt instantly sick, like it was not mist at all but poison gas. I drug myself to my feet as Piston pointed a long dirty finger toward me. "And to think I was going to let you live."

But I wasn't paying all that much attention to Piston at the moment. My eyes were on the basin. At first, I thought that was where the mist was coming from, but then I realized I was wrong. The mist wasn't flowing from the basin; it was flowing up and into it, as if somewhere someone had flipped a switch on a vacuum.

Faster and faster it went, until in one soundless whoosh the last wisp disappeared over the edge.

For the barest of seconds, there was silence. And then, the roar. A column of viscous liquid, like oil, but somehow thicker and darker, erupted from the heart of the basin. Piston stumbled backward, and Tonto shrieked. I followed the flood up, up, up into the eternal darkness above. I supposed that if the temple had a ceiling, it was striking it, but we didn't have long to wonder. Down it came again, but it did not crash to the floor. Instead, it gathered above the basin itself, swirling in a great, black ball that pulsated with life.

"Piston!" Tonto cried. "Piston, what's going on?"

But Piston had no answers. We were all the same, standing witness to an event we were never meant to see. Then something happened I could not have expected — things got *way* worse.

The black sphere ceased to be a black sphere anymore. It bulged and split, and I thought I saw feet, hands, claws. Then there was no question. Some sort of beast was forming before us. It was not emerging from the dark sphere. They were one and the same.

Hog stared up at the birth of that hideous thing, and I suspect his grip slipped on the girl, because she did what any sane person would have done in that moment—she ran. No one tried to stop her. We might as well have been held to the spot by steel spikes. She might have made it, too, but just as she passed me, a whip-like arm of black ichor shot forth from the heart of the beast and wrapped around her throat. She gave a cry, tiny, more startled than painful, as if she simply could not believe this was happening to her. Then in one great jerk that may well have broken her neck then and there, she snapped back into the midst of the living void.

The beast took a step forward and I understood that it intended to make the girl's fate the fate of us all. I glanced from Piston to Hog to Tonto. They looked like children, scared little kids. The tough demeanor, the ruse they played on people smaller and weaker than them, was gone. They saw the end of all things standing before them. Or at least, the end of all *their* things. The beast took another step. The entrance to the temple was behind me. If I took off, I might be able to make it while that monster was busy with the others.

But hell, I couldn't do that. And I say again, it's not that I'm some kind of hero. Truth be told I'm as scared of things that go bump in the night as the next guy. I just have a guilty streak, and if I'd let those poor sons-of-bitches die, I knew I'd regret it someday. True, they weren't worth much, scum of the earth and all, and I figured they could add that girl's death to their list of sins. But together, the three of them might just have enough good in them to be worth one of me. And a rodeo clown is kinda like a secret service agent. It's his job to take the horn, no matter how piss-poor the guy he's defending.

Piston, Hog, and Tonto hadn't moved half an inch, but the beast—I don't really know what else to call it—was walking or gliding or floating or whatever toward them. I raised my stump hand in the air and hollered my best imitation of the Rebel Yell. Great Granddaddy would have been proud.

"Over here you bloated cloud of cow fart!"

Alright, so it wasn't my best insult, but it worked. The thing didn't much have a head, and I felt more than saw it turn, but I knew I had its full attention.

"You're facing an honest-to-God rodeo clown, a card-carrying member of the Brotherhood of the American Bullfighter, local 229, and that's what I do. I fight bulls twice your size and half as ugly and I'm not one bit afraid of you!"

And like a bull in the ring, it charged me. It came at me full on, what looked like liquid obsidian, if such a thing is even possible, forming into a mass like a locomotive. I let it come, right until it was almost upon me, and then I simply stepped to the side. It roared past, slamming into the wall of the temple.

"We call that the *pasodoble*," I said. "It's Spanish."

The thing rolled over on itself, like a turning bull, and thrust at me again. So I stepped to the other side and it slid past.

"That's the *doble*!" I hollered at it. It paused in place, floating above the ground. It no longer looked like some kind of Minotaur or classic monster out of a bad horror movie, but like a black orb of impenetrable darkness. I spread my legs and crouched, a linebacker waiting for the snap. In an instant a thick tendril of oil shot out at me, just like it had at the girl earlier. I dove forward, rolling underneath it and out of the way.

"That all you got?" I yelled as the tentacle recoiled back into the mass. But I was already breathing heavy, and I wasn't precisely sure just how much *I* had left. I spared a glance at the Three Stooges. To my utter amazement, they still stood there, rooted to the spot with their mouths hanging open to the floor, and I even thought I saw drool seeping out of Tonto's. Probably not an unusual occurrence.

I didn't have time to say anything as a large arm the size of a telephone poll swung around toward me. I made a guess and lunged like I was going to barrel roll again. The column of ichor crashed to the ground and swept across it. I'd guessed right. Instead of rolling I leapt as far and high as I could, clear over it, landing on the other side on my feet. I ran, knowing the arm was probably swinging back even then.

I pointed at Piston and yelled, "Get through the door, you assholes!" Finally understanding sprung back into his eyes. He turned and said something to the other two, but I didn't hear him. The roar of swirling air and massive movement filled my ears. By the time I glanced back, it was on top of me.

"Time to make the rounds," I said to myself. I jumped to the side, right as the form almost touched me—and something told me that even the slightest contact meant death—and it slid past. But this time not all the way, just as I had anticipated. Instead it flipped on itself, attempting to double back on me. As it turned, I turned, and now we were locked in a dance of death, like a dog chasing its tail where the tail was me. Out of the corner of my eye I saw the three bikers running for the crack. In a few moments, they would be there. They'd be free. And, well, I'd be dead. I couldn't turn forever, and with no one to distract it, I'd never escape.

Then something changed. It sensed, or perhaps it saw, the three running. It stopped turning so abruptly that I almost ran into it, but instead I fell to the ground before it. It formed a wall and, like a wave rolling away from me, arched across the chamber. It waterfalled down in front of the entrance way, blocking the only exit. The three men ground to a halt, Hog slipping and tumbling.

The wave crashed down upon him, swallowing him up. He didn't even have time to scream.

"Shit," I said, pushing myself up. There was a fairly hefty stone beside me and I picked it up, unsure of what good it would do. I was exhausted, but I began to run toward the inky, living wall. Piston backed away, his hands up as if he was trying to explain himself to an angry lover. When he turned to run, another tentacle shot from the mass and looped around his right leg. With one giant lurch, it had him hanging in the air, suspended thirty feet above the ground. He screamed like a child, high-pitched and urgent, begging to be released, for whatever held him to just let him go. So, it did. His keening reached its peak and then was silenced, replaced by the crunch of his head splitting open on the ground, like a walnut smashed by a hammer. The creature slid forward over the body and the growing pool of blood, and when it withdrew, the floor was clear and clean.

Tonto was running toward me as I was running toward him, his eyes filled with madness and fear. I wasn't sure exactly what we were going to do or where we were going to go, but I figured I'd die fighting, and maybe screaming, too. Tonto was almost to me when I heard a sound like a whip-crack and saw a serpent-like band wrap around his throat. His eyes went wide, and in another instant I knew the beast would have him. I reared back and threw the stone as hard as I could. To my amazement, it struck the tentacle and cleaved it in two. The larger part withdrew; the smaller fell to the ground where it exploded into black smoke upon contact. I was exuberant, and just as I was about to let out a massive war whoop, I looked up at Tonto. His hands went to his neck. His eyes were filled with fear and confusion. And then, I shit you not, he actually giggled. Right before his head tilted to the side and fell with a splat to the ground.

So that was it. They were all dead, and I was next. The black curtain before me expanded. Its height reached into the infinite darkness above, its width all the way to each wall. I knew then it had been toying with me all along. It could have had me at any point. Could have had any of us. But for some reason known only to whatever mad intelligence guided it, it had waited till now to show its full glory. It began moving forward, and I stumbled back. Past one set of columns and then another. Eventually I'd run out of room and it would take me, but I was in no hurry to see that happen, so I kept walking backward toward the altar.

Then the wall stopped. It hung there, dividing the room in half, preventing me from my only means of escape, but it came no further. For a moment I wondered why, but then I became aware of another presence. A heard a sound, as of a slapping upon the ground, a great girth moving in jerking steps. I turned to face it, whatever it was, whatever new horror was to meet my eyes. It was not what I expected.

In my younger years, I'd gigged my share of frogs in the southern swamps. I now repented my youthful indiscretions.

I'll explain what I saw, but the best I can tell you is this—it appeared to be a giant frog, a great toad complete with massive belly and globular eyes that looked as if they longed for nothing more than sleep. It was covered with brown fur, which might have been disconcerting on an actual frog but somehow seemed perfectly reasonable here. Its mouth opened slightly, and the tip of a tongue darted out. I fully expected to hear the mightiest ribbit ever to issue forth in the history of the world. But when he spoke, it was only in my mind that I heard it.

"Bullfighter, I am the one who sleeps. You have awakened me from my slumber."

"I'm sorry," I whispered, almost questioningly. My mind could not process what I was seeing and hearing.

"No matter. You are not of the cult. The others should have known better."

He moved toward me, his massive splayed feet crashing down upon the temple floor with every step.

"It is a strange thing. I knew another, of your kind, long ago, in a very different place from this. He was a thief, a master at his art, whose name is now lost to the shrouds of time. But not his memory, and not his soul."

He raised himself up to meet my eyes, even though one of his was the size of my entire head.

"Twice our paths crossed, the thief and I. And twice I let him go. I promised him there would not be a third time. And now, I sense some of him in you."

I swallowed hard, but my mouth was so dry that there was nothing there to swallow.

"I see into you. There is courage there, unlike most of your brethren. Enough, I think, to make me overlook my promise, oh Satampra Zeiros."

Upon hearing that name, something stirred within me, something I had not known was there.

"Go," it said, "and see that you do not come back."

It turned from me then and began to shuffle away. I glanced behind me and watched as the great black curtain split down the middle and opened. I looked back at the other beast as it went, the giant frog, and for reasons unknown, I opened my mouth to speak.

"What do I call you?" I asked.

It stopped and turned to look upon me. This time when it spoke its voice rang out with such force that it drew the consciousness from me, and it didn't come back until I woke up, inexplicably, on the main street of the abandoned town above, Sam and Jake shaking my shoulders and screaming at me like they thought I was dead. The beast, the god, didn't say much. Just one word…

His own name.

"TSATHOGGUA!"

What the Dead Can Tell

"The problem with you Americans is that you take everything so seriously."

Crowley poured another glass of vodka—the good stuff—and slid it across to Toporov. The man's hands were as steady as the dead when he grasped it.

"Don't you think things like this are worth getting serious over?" Crowley asked.

The old Communist looked at him and grinned. "I get serious over things I can change." He raised the glass, said something in Russian, and downed it.

There was a loud buzz and the door opened. In walked Stephenson. Uniform crisp and smart, mouth fixed in a permanent scowl. "We getting anywhere?"

"Not yet."

Stephenson dropped a file folder onto the table, stamped *Top Secret* and entitled "Golden Halo."

"Latest satellite images on the site. You better get to it. Shit's falling apart fast, and the energy spikes are off the charts. Brief me when you're done here."

Crowley examined the photographs as the door buzzed and Stephenson slipped back outside. The site was hot alright, and time was running short.

Toporov sat quietly, heavily lidded eyes locked on Crowley. He licked his lips, normally a sign of nervousness but in this case probably not. Toporov wasn't the kind of man to indulge in nerves. *Maybe in the Lubiyanka,* Crowley thought. *Maybe on his knees over a blood-stained grate with a Makarov jammed into the base of his skull. He might be scared then.*

But not here, not in Washington, D.C., where diplomatic protocols and common, civilized, western decency protected him from such things. At least for now. Might not for much longer, if things kept getting worse.

"I am not sure what you want from me, Special Agent Crowley. I am not sure what you believe I can give you."

Crowley grinned, falsely. "Come now, Colonel. We've known each other long enough to skip the bullshit. Golden Halo has been compromised. You know it and I know it. Things have gone to hell in Moscow. The Wall fell and now the old empire is going with it. Smart guy like you can see what comes next. This is no time for hardliners. Evolve or die, that's always been the way of the world. Time to crawl out of the ocean and stand on your own two feet."

"And crawling out of the ocean means turning over state secrets to you, no?"

"There is no state, Toporov. The Soviet Union is dead, or it's damn near close. It's crumbling even as we speak. In a week the party'll be outlawed and they'll be lining loyalists up in front of walls and shooting them. You know how this thing always goes. Meet the new boss, same as the old boss. You should just consider yourself lucky we picked you up when we did and took you into protective custody."

"Ah yes, protective custody. How could I forget." And then, lowering his gaze, "I thought we were skipping the bullshit, special agent. Perhaps if you could get me a pack of cigarettes we could talk. The ones with the cowboy, the Marlboro man, if you don't mind."

Crowley reached into his jacket pocket and lobbed a pack of reds onto the table. "See, we're not so different after all. I even got your favorite color." Toporov removed a cigarette which Crowley lit before taking one of his own. "So let's get down to business and I'll be straight with you if you're straight with me. We've had Golden Halo under aerial and then orbital surveillance for about as long as we've had aerial and orbital surveillance. We've got no idea what it is, even though we've tried to find out—and there are several gold stars on the wall at Langley that tidily sum up our failures. When the shit hit the fan in Moscow, Soviet troops abandoned their positions in mass. From Chernobyl to Vladivostok. What's left of your central command deployed Spetznaz to protect vulnerable nuclear sites, and that's good. But Golden Halo has always been protected by the best of the best, and now even they've booked it, and that's bad."

Crowley paused for a moment, let Toporov's thoughts hang in the void. An old interrogator's tactic, and he was surprised to see it work. The Russian broke.

"Christ," he spat, and when he brought his hand up to rub the bridge of his nose, it shook. "It's finally happened."

"What, Colonel? What has happened?"

Toporov licked his lips, and this time Crowley thought that he *was* nervous, more nervous than he would be even if he were down on his knees in the basement of KGB headquarters.

"Every year, around the world," he said, "people go missing. They disappear. By the thousands. Even here. Even in your country. Tens of thousands of children alone." He snapped his fingers. "Poof. Now most can be explained, most mysteries solved, of course. If they were not, if they all stayed a mystery, perhaps someone would notice. Perhaps they would wonder. But even as it is, there remain those mysteries that are *never* solved. Do you know of what I speak?"

Crowley nodded, cautiously. In all honesty he wasn't entirely sure what Toporov was getting at, but he figured there was no harm in playing along. "Sure. Of course. There's a whole wing of the Bureau that does nothing but look for the missing."

"But they don't always find them, do they?"

The agent shrugged. "Not all of them. Like you said, some of them are just gone. But you can't dwell on it. Some things you just can't know."

"Ah, but you are wrong, special agent. Someone does know. Someone always knows. If nothing else, the person knows. Do you ever wonder what the missing know? What the dead can tell? What they have seen that you have not? What mysteries the final moments of their lives revealed? I wonder that sometimes. And I wonder if one of the answers to such mysteries is in the place you call Golden Halo. Is there a reason you call it that, or is it random?"

Crowley shook his head. "No, not random. Stupid maybe. They named it after the color of the clouds that sometimes circle the mountain. Apparently, they glow yellow."

Toporov chuckled, and Crowley shivered. The way the old Russian laughed. He was a study in control, but in his laughter was a touch of madness, a sign that behind the façade of calm was a man ready to collapse. "Of course they do. What other color would it be?" He waved his hand, as if dismissing the thought. "We do not call it Golden Halo of course. We have a Russian name for it, though in the tongue of the natives. Holatchahl. The Mountain of the Dead."

"That's a little dramatic, don't you think?"

"Dramatic? Accurate? I cannot say. As I said, it is the name the Mansi, the natives, gave it. They do not go there, under any circumstances. Even though they still live in the area and have for millennia. Unlike your nation, we did not slaughter all the indigenous people. Even if we did try. More vodka, please. My mouth is dry from talking."

"So the Mountain of the Dead?" said Crowley as he poured. "Is it some sort of military facility?"

Toporov hesitated, then met Crowley's eyes. "It is, but not one that we built."

Crowley cocked his head, looked at him sideways. "I'm not sure I follow your meaning."

"It is as I said it is. Something built the facility long ago. We do not know who."

"Some*thing*?"

"I chose my words deliberately, special agent. It was not an error in translation. Imagine a hole in the earth, on the mountain's eastern slope. But imagine it sealed with a metal cap, the metallurgy of which you have never seen before and will not see again. Not that we didn't learn from it. Our submarines dive deeper than yours for a reason."

"Go on," said Crowley. He'd started to take notes now, even if they read like the diary of a madman.

"It was not known to us until 1940. The Nazis discovered it."

"Wait, what? The Nazis?"

Toporov nodded. "They had their Thule SS guards combing the world for ancient artifacts, sources of power. God only knows how they found out about this one. It is in no Russian text that I have ever read, neither ancient nor modern. From rumors and innuendo, I suppose, the way the Nazis did most things. Everything built on lies and suppositions, but sometimes lies turn out to be true. I was there when we found them, only a 16-year-old boy from Riga. My family fled the Germans as they came. I was the only one to survive, and I swore I would have my revenge." Toporov's eyes drifted off, above and behind Crowley's shoulder, somewhere into the past. The interrogator let him sit, ruminate, think about the story. Whatever he was about to reveal would not be a lie. Crowley'd done this long enough to know that. But he could not wait forever.

"And did you get it that day?"

The question broke Toporov from his trance and he looked back at Crowley. "Oh no, special agent. Those poor bastards were far beyond any harm I might do them."

The door buzzed, Stephenson again. He stepped inside, holding another folder in his hand. And like Crowley's fifth grade math teacher, he looked at him over the rim of his glasses. "Uh, Agent Crowley, can I speak with you for a second." Crowley felt like he was just getting to the good part, but he couldn't exactly say no. He held up an index finger—the universal sign for "hold that thought"—and left Toporov at the table, smoking another cigarette.

"What's up?"

Stephenson's permanent scowl darkened. "What in the holy hell are you two talking about in there anyway?"

"I'm getting his story."

"The one about ancient aliens and Nazis?"

"I don't believe there was any mention of aliens."

"Just consider that he may be playing you for time, and that's time we do not have." He smacked the folder into Crowley's chest. "Newest satellite sweep. The Russians are still running like scared children. Why, we don't know. Maybe it's a coincidence, maybe we've got another Chernobyl on our hands that just happened to coincide with the greatest victory for the West since V-E Day. But whatever the case may be, somebody else is on their way to the site."

Crowley grabbed the folder, flipped it open to the images. He furrowed his brow, confused. He'd expected to see trucks, tankers, vehicles to carry away the loot—nuclear and conventional—to be sold on the black market to the highest bidder. Instead he saw men on horseback, following a single individual who appeared to be carrying nothing but a long staff.

"What am I looking at, Stephenson?"

"Beats the hell out of me. Why don't you ask the Russian?" He said, gesturing at Toporov who sat, arms crossed and leaned back in his chair, with the sort of self-satisfied smugness that every interrogator hates. The door buzzed, and Stephenson left, but not before making it clear, with his eyes alone, that Crowley had better find out something useful, and fast.

"In point of fact, I am not Russian. I am Latvian."

Crowley ignored him.

"So here's the thing, Colonel," Crowley said as he sat back down across from Toporov, "I'm running out of time. We don't know what's at the site, but the energy spikes are like nothing we've ever seen before. There are some guys up in Strategic Command that are more of the nuke first, ask questions later types, and they figure with the government collapsing, we can probably get away with it, too, without turning the entire eastern seaboard into black glass. Me, I'm not so sure. So I'd really like you to tell me the truth, and not some bullshit story."

"It is not bullshit, my friend."

"Then how did a pack of Nazis get that far into the Ural Mountains in the middle of the war?"

"The Thule SS were quite resourceful. It was nothing for them to accomplish, I can assure you."

"But you said you couldn't hurt them?"

"Of course not. They were already dead. But it was more than that. Much more. In truth, we had never seen the likes of it. We know now the harm that radiation poisoning can bring. Bleeding from every orifice. Hair falling out. Skin burned as if by fire. Flaking away, in the worst cases. Your body, rotting from the inside. It is a very unpleasant way to die. But of course, at the time your people had not introduced the world to the horrors of nuclear fire so what we saw that day appeared to us to be the vengeance of an angry god, one that we did not recognize from our Bibles. But even knowing what we do now, I cannot imagine how it must have happened. The amount of energy that must have surged up from the pit at the moment of awakening to leave them in that state, surrounding the seal that they had removed."

"Slow down, Toporov, you're confusing me."

The old Latvian began to cackle. "As if slowing down would allow you to understand. As if your mind—or any man's mind— could catalogue or categorize what I have seen. As if you could put it into any order that fits with your understanding of the world. No, my friend. I have been mad from the moment I stepped foot on that mountain. I have known that for a long time, but I accept it now for it is only in madness that such a thing can have any sanity at all." To Crowley's confusion, he simply held up his hands in surrender. "But I digress and your time is running short. So please, don't interrupt.

"We found the men surrounding the open hole. It had not been open for long, and beside them was the metal seal that they had undoubtedly been the ones to shove aside. We could not tell, of course, how long they had been dead, but from the positioning of their bodies we could speculate. We believed that they had died shortly after—very shortly after—they had pried up the seal and pushed it to the side. They had not died quickly, but death had preoccupied them, if you take my meaning, and they did not move from where they fell save to thrash about in the ecstasy of their agony.

"My thought was to replace the seal and flee. To this day I believe that was the prudent course. In fact, I have no doubt of it. But being a young man of low rank I kept that thought to myself, though I was heartened when an older soldier who had seen much in the way of war voiced those same sentiments. But our lieutenant was a party apparatchik of the pure faith, and he believed that whatever had killed the fascists must be a weapon, one that the motherland could seize to throw back the enemy from our borders. It is as it always is, I suppose, with every war and with every people. God is always on your side, even if as a good Communist you don't believe in a god. But I can promise you this, special agent. There are *gods*. But they do not care for you or me or for the petty concerns of the insignificant human vermin that team upon the face of this planet. They do not care at all.

"But our lieutenant, brave or stupid or both, would not hear of it. He would go down into the pit to see if he could discover the source of the astonishing power that had killed our enemies. There were stairs, of a sort—if you were a giant, perhaps—leading down into the depths. And a great yellow light."

"A light? What kind of light?"

"We didn't know at first. Do not misunderstand me. It did not allow us to *see*. Rather, it was in the depths, circular, as if deep below there was a single source of illumination. We could not imagine what could make such a light, or why it glowed below while leaving the path at the surface bathed in darkness. I see the doubt in your eyes, and I do not blame you. It is a thing that must be seen, not explained. You did not see, so you cannot understand.

"We begged the lieutenant not to go, but he rebuked us for our cowardice, even if it was on his own behalf. He took a flashlight and descended, assuring us that he would return soon and that we would all share in the glory. We watched him, a ball of light in the darkness, as he clambered down the mighty steps, sliding on his belly to the edge and then dropping down. His return would be even more difficult, I thought, as he would have to pull himself up again and again."

Toporov turned wistful, picked up the faded bottle of vodka and poured another shot. Crowley admired his fortitude.

"But," he said, raising the glass, "we need not have worried about such trivialities." He downed the shot, fortifying himself for whatever was to come next.

"Down he went, growing closer to the source of illumination. We thought that whatever made it must have been enormous, given how with every step the light our comrade bore grew smaller and smaller until finally it faded away altogether. Just imagine the depths. Imagine what it must have taken to build such a staircase. The unfathomable technical skill. And there, in the midst of the Ural Mountains! But such thoughts were for later. We stared into the void. We awaited some sign. We soon received it. It came like a rush of wind that roared up from below and burst forth into the world. And on it rode a scream, a scream of such horror and terror and pain that I cannot imagine it even now, even though I heard it with my own ears. I tell you this, special agent, I have been on battlefields where men died cruelly, befitting the genius and brutality of our species, but I have never heard a man make that sound."

"Did you go in after him?"

"I think we might have, though who can say for sure with the fear we felt at that moment? But we didn't have much time to think on it. Not when we saw the truth. The light...well, it was no light. We couldn't deny it anymore.

"Not after that great eye blinked.

"Whatever sanity we had left broke then, and in a delirium of terror we shoved the seal back in place, though we could not know if it would hold. We could not know if in breaking it the Germans had robbed it of all its power. But it did hold, for the moment at least, though it could not cover the sound of the titanic pounding from below.

"We reported exactly what happened to our headquarters. And they believed us. Don't look so surprised. Our people have always been more willing to accept the strange and unusual than yours. Within hours, the mountain crawled with Soviet troops. It became a research station, as our scientists struggled to understand what sort of being waited beneath it. Waited for another opportunity to make its escape. And we wondered what it meant for mankind or the evolution of this planet, what it portended for other deep places around the world, or what it said of the things that lived here before man first raised his eyes to the stars.

"Death followed that place. No one could work there for more than a few months, lest they go insane. Soldiers and scientists alike hated it. Civilians were, of course, forbidden, though sometimes they would come anyway, always to their doom. I remember once that nine hikers tried to climb the mountain. By the time they were buried, not even their families could recognize the bodies. So it does not surprise me that its guardians are abandoning Temnaya Zvezda...or that the thing that lies beneath it has chosen this moment to escape."

"What are you trying to tell me, Toporov, that this is the end of the world or something? Cause that's not going to happen. We aren't going to let it happen. I've got missiles in Turkey pointed at Golden Halo and I can atomize your little mystery facility in the blink of an eye."

Toporov broke into laughter, and Crowley thought him truly mad.

"My dear friend, you believe that a creature that has spanned space and time can be destroyed? It would bathe in your nuclear fire and rise like a phoenix to cover the world. No, the only hope for us all..." he reached across the table and snatched the latest satellite photo, "is that those men reach their destination, and that something of the old wisdom remains with them. The wisdom of this age has no power there. They will write the next chapter. Pray that it is not the last."

And so it was that as millions sat with rapt attention before their televisions as an empire fell, another story was unfolding on a remote mountain top, a story known to only a few, and even they were never sure what was truth and what was fiction. All they could say, in whispers over too many drinks in dimly lit bars, was that on that mountain top, men from a forgotten people stood against an ancient evil and defeated it.

For now.

Beneath the Shadow of the Hills

"Let's go to Maine," Maggie said. "We'll watch the leaves change and get shitfaced. Just like old times."

"Back in the 'old times,' we never watched the leaves change."

"Then we'll get shitfaced just like old times and watch the leaves change because somehow we turned into old ladies." Maggie giggled, her eyes sparkling above that mischievous smile Carol had always loved. Forty-five years old and Maggie hadn't changed since she was a teenager.

"And Amy?"

Maggie rolled her eyes and leaned back in one of the camp chairs she'd used to populate her spacious deck. Her glass of wine swirled in great circles and threatened to attain escape velocity. "You know Amy. She's up for anything."

In this case, maybe. Carol knew that both Amy and Maggie would do just about anything to cheer her up, to drag her out of this funk. Matt had been dead for six months and people were ready for her to move on. Only Maggie, and maybe Amy, knew just how hard it had been. For the first month she'd hardly gotten out of bed, and when she did, it was like she was floating above and behind herself, like she was a ghost and a zombie all at once. Her spirit watching her rotting corpse shuffle through life, what was left of it, at least.

Chrissy, her daughter, hadn't been able to stand it. But she had college as an excuse and was able to leave her mother behind without too much guilt. Maggie and Amy couldn't get away. They'd always been there, always would be there.

Now Maggie had a plan. Get Carol out of the house and back into the world, starting with a vacation. But of all things, leaf peeping?

Carol looked out over the back of Maggie's deck and down the little residential street that didn't seem like it belonged on the outskirts of D.C. That's why Maggie had chosen it, of course. In the old days, Maggie had lived fast and loose, and she never would have wanted to be anywhere other than the heart of it all. An attorney, she had worked long hours and partied even longer. There had been occasions when her colleagues would have sworn that she was wearing the same outfit as the day before, and more often than not they were right. She had never married, never had kids or even contemplated the possibility. There had been whispers that she might be a lesbian, and more than once she and Carol and Amy had laughed about that over a bottle—or several—of wine. Maggie liked men; she just never liked them twice.

So when a few years back Maggie had bought this place on the edge of Rockville on a quiet Maryland street, Carol and Amy had been surprised. Maggie had laughed it off, of course, but Carol wondered if maybe she regretted how her life had gone. Forty-five was by no means old, not these days at least. But Maggie acted as though it was, as if whatever life she had lived up to that point was all that she ever would.

A gust of wind came swirling down the empty street, carrying with it the chill touch of the coming fall. It was imminent now. Summer had officially ended, but in Washington the heat of the near-South held on stubbornly, refusing to bow to the calendar. But Carol could feel it. The days would grow short, the nights cold, life would flee, and dead winter would have the city in its grip.

"Yeah," she said. "OK. Let's do it."

*　*　*

A week later they were off for two weekends and the days in between of girl time, drinking, and probably pot if Maggie had her way. They took Amy's car, a big SUV Amy didn't need now that her two kids were at Notre Dame.

Amy and Carol had married young, straight out of college. Carol had Chrissy and that was it, the one girl's birth coming as close as seemingly possible in this modern world to taking Carol's life. Amy had twins, Hunter and Haley, virtually inseparable even to this day. But now both women had joined Maggie in her empty nest. Amy's ex, David, wasn't dead, but he might as well be.

"Alright, bitches," Amy said as they climbed in. Ever tanned, she wore too-big sunglasses and enough bangles to satisfy a Bollywood dancer. "Let's go peep the hell out of some leaves." They all got a good laugh from that.

They went to New York City first, spent a night on Broadway on Maggie's dime and shopped and drank too much and slept in the next day. On to Boston, where whatever grip summer still held on DC was but a distant memory. Boston, so bright and vibrant in the summer days, was already beginning to dull. The ironclad clouds gathering above the Pru portended autumn rain, and the wind that whipped down Beacon Hill held no trace of warmth.

So they ate littlenecks and hot clam chowder and dreamt of Maine. The next day they paid the toll at the border and crossed over, on the way to the cabin on the lake that Maggie's parents had owned for as long as Carol knew her, and which now belonged to her.

Maggie's grandfather—Papa Masterson she had called him before he disappeared into the woods they would now traverse, the victim of dementia being the generally accepted theory—had built the cabin on property the family owned on the shores of Sentinel Lake. It was a large plot, covering the whole northern side of Sentinel and well into the hills beyond. They had no neighbors, not for miles by road or water. Which made it the perfect place for a getaway—or for a young and wild Maggie to grab the bull of life by the horns and ride it.

She'd lost her virginity there to a scared kid from the all-boys school that served as Hawthorne Academy's complement. The event had lasted approximately thirty-seven seconds, she had once told Carol and Amy, before ending messily and unsatisfactorily— for Maggie at least. "I teased him too much before," she had said a couple years later, the three of them laughing hysterically over a bottle of tequila and a game of Never-Have-I-Ever. "But don't worry, I've learned my lesson."

The cabin was the first place they'd got drunk, the first place they'd smoked pot, and the only place they'd tried Ecstasy, a bit of experimentation that was never repeated. It lay down a one lane dirt road that wound through the woods, hugging the shore of the lake, even if you could only occasionally glimpse the water through the dense foliage. Amy took the road at a solid 50 miles per hour, regardless of the fact that the early autumn sun was already dipping below the horizon, rendering the blind curves even more so. Carol did not complain. No one was coming, and in truth, she was anxious to get to the cabin.

She'd been here dozens of times. But always in the summer, with its wet heat and its long, lazy days and its warm winds racing across the cool lake. It felt different now, the shadows somehow longer and deeper and darker. And she wondered if it was the season or her own mood that had changed. Amy and Maggie were doing their best, but what if even this place was cursed for her?

Carol didn't say much on the way. Amy was a teacher at a high school in northern Virginia and spent most of the drive railing against the "bleach-blond bimbo with the pushed up tits" who was screwing the assistant principal. Maggie, and even Carol, laughed. They did not mention that Amy herself had been screwing the assistant principal less than a year earlier.

But all conversation had fallen away as they approached the cabin. Carol didn't know why, but it also didn't matter. She preferred the silence.

It was a cabin in the loosest sense of the word. Two stories, modern in every way, with indoor plumbing and central heating. Maggie's parents liked the illusion of the outdoors more than its realities.

The trio pulled into the drive just as dusk was turning to full dark. Maggie made margaritas while Amy rolled joints and Carol tried to convince herself that this was how it always was. That the cabin did not feel more cavernous than before, the outdoors more foreboding. In their previous visits, they'd spent as much time outside as in, sitting on the porch, watching the stars, taking shots and telling funny stories which were at least half true.

Carol would not go out there now, no matter what her friends might say. The cool air gave her an excuse, albeit a flimsy one. The darkness seemed to gather about the little cabin, and the fire Maggie had built only made the wall of black night just beyond the window panes more impenetrable.

Maggie poured them all a drink and plopped on the couch. She grabbed the remote and turned off the television over the fireplace that Amy had tuned to a reality show about the perils of one woman dating 25 men.

"Hey," Amy whined. "I was watching that."

"We didn't come here to watch television."

Amy grabbed her margarita from Maggie. "Speak for yourself. I'm on vacation."

"Exactly," Maggie said. She grinned mischievously. It was a look Carol had seen many times before. It seldom ended well for anyone involved.

She walked behind the couch and reached down, and from the rustle of fabric Carol could tell she was uncovering something. When she popped up again, the grin had not faded.

"Ready?" she said. Up came a box, long and rectangular. The words written on the top almost made Carol gasp. "I found it last time I was here."

"A Ouija board?" Amy said, her lilting voice tinged with more than a hint of mockery. "What, are we in high school?" As if to make the point, she lit one of the joints, and took a deep drag. Maggie visibly deflated.

"Oh come on," she said. "It'll be fun!"

Carol didn't say what she thought. She thought it was morbid, and inappropriate, and maybe even slightly disrespectful. She had come here to forget about death. It was not a game to her anymore. It was real and terrible and not to be messed with. But she didn't say any of that. Maggie was the leader, Amy was the rebel. They figured things out and Carol went along. She was the follower. That was the way it had always been. When together they were in boarding school, when they went to college, when they moved to DC. That was always it.

Amy collapsed back on the couch. "Oh for shit's sake. Alright, whatever."

"Great. I'll get the lights."

With every switch she flipped, the room descended further into darkness. Soon, only the flickering light of the fire provided any illumination. Maggie came back to the couch and reached inside her bag, removing three candles—the kind in tall, glass containers Carol had often seen slapped with images of saints on the side. These were plain, and when Maggie lit them, they seemed to burn brighter than Carol would have expected.

"You remember how to do this, right?"

Amy rolled her eyes and put her fingers on her side of the planchette. Maggie took her side. Both women looked to Carol. She did not hesitate. She wanted her friends to see her strength, not her weakness.

"Alright, ladies," Maggie said. "You know how this works. Any question is fair game. Around and round we go!"

They began to move the planchette in a figure eight, faster and faster, "to warm up the board," or so Maggie had told them. Then Carol began to feel some resistance, and gradually the little triangle of wood ground to a halt. Maggie looked up at her, with eyes that sparkled in the firelight.

"OK," she said, "who goes first?"

"Will Maggie ever stop being such a slut?"

"Hey!"

"Everything's fair game right?"

The planchette swung around, and whatever else could be said for it, Carol was just along for the ride. It made a wide arc before stopping on YES.

"See, I'm settling down in my old age," Maggie said. They all giggled, and for a moment, Carol was actually having fun.

"Will Amy ever get laid again?" Carol said, surprised at her own self. The tequila was taking hold. The planchette slid upward and then came swooping back down before stopping on NO.

"Now you're just being a bunch of bitches," Amy spat.

"I'm not moving it!" Maggie squealed.

"Me neither," added Carol.

"Whatever."

The planchette sat quietly, waiting.

"Do you have a name?" Amy asked.

The oracle slid over. YES.

"Will you tell us?"

NO.

Amy looked up at Maggie and Carol and scowled. "What, neither of you can come up with a decent name?"

"I told you," Maggie said, "I'm not moving it."

"Just ask another question," Carol said.

"Initials then?"

The planchette swung to the S, and then over to an N.

Amy's brow creased and her nose wrinkled. "S-N?"

Maggie rolled her eyes. "Oh good God, this is boring."

"Then you ask the questions!"

"I will. Alright," she said, and that mischievous sparkle came back into her eyes. "OK, let's get serious. Do you know everything?"

The oracle slid to YES.

"Cocky bastard," Amy said. Maggie ignored her.

"Then tell me which one of us bitches is going to kick the bucket first?"

Even with the heat of the fire at her back, Carol shuddered. "Maggie..." she almost whimpered.

"It's just for fun, remember. Come on," she said to the board, "tell me."

For a moment the oracle sat silent, while they sat on the edge of their seat. And for a moment, Carol thought maybe there would be no answer, that they'd put away the stupid game and drink more tequila and smoke more weed and wish they were twenty years younger. Then, the planchette began to move.

It circled in broad swoops, diving and rising, and the sound of its padded legs on the wooden board drilled into Carol's mind. For a second the oracle passed over the M, and seemed to slow. But it did not stop. It sped up, in fact, and circled around again, moving so quickly that Carol almost lost her grip. Then it slowed, almost to a crawl. The A came within its glass. It slowed… slowed… slowed… but it never quite stopped. It swooped up, flew down, and made a hard right turn.

Carol let go of the oracle and flipped the board into the air. Maggie and Amy were too shocked to react.

"This is stupid. I'm going to bed."

She had already slammed the door of her bedroom behind her by the time Maggie called out her name. Carol couldn't hear her. All she could think was that the planchette had been heading directly toward the C.

* * *

The next morning Carol got up, showered, and put on her hiking clothes before she went down for breakfast. Maggie had mentioned wanting to explore the woods behind the cabin. It was the only good idea she'd had on this trip, as far as Carol was concerned. She could smell the bacon cooking before she saw Amy in the kitchen bent over the stove. Maggie was drinking coffee and reading the paper. She looked up when Carol rounded the corner.

"Hey, kiddo," she said, smiling. "You ready to hit the trails?"

"Sure. But I'm starving."

It was as if the night before hadn't happened. They ate bacon and pancakes and fried eggs and talked about nothing in particular.

When breakfast was finished, they filled their backpacks with bottles of water and trail mix and stepped out into the crisp morning.

It was quiet on the lake. During the summer, the water would be covered in craft of every kind, from pontoon boats which served as little more than floating bars to speedboats that flew across the waves dragging adventurous college students behind them. But today, there was hardly anyone, only a lone fishing boat on the far end, so distant that even the gentle lapping of the waves caused it to disappear every few seconds.

Maggie led them into the woods, and Carol had to admit that the tapestry of multicolored leaves that clung to dying branches and carpeted the forest floor was striking. It might not have been the trip she would have chosen, but that didn't mean she wasn't impressed.

"It's beautiful, isn't it? My parents used to bring me up here every fall."

"I didn't know that," Amy said.

"Yeah, it was before I started school. When I was just a little girl. After that, we only came in the summer."

A breeze played the music of the season among the limbs of the trees, just a kiss of coming winter riding on it. Birds winged above the forested canopy heading south to warmer climes. She couldn't see them, but Carol could hear whatever creatures called the woodlands home scurrying beneath and among the fallen leaves.

"I'm glad we came here," Carol said. "This is perfect."

"So where are we going?" Amy asked.

The path had cut across a small stream and had now begun to ascend.

"Bald Mountain," said Maggie.

Amy and Carol shared a curious glance.

"Bald Mountain?" Amy said. "What's that?"

"Don't worry, chubs. It's more of a hill really."

Amy let the insult pass. It was easy for her. That she was the fittest—and the thinnest—of the group was beyond dispute. "Yeah," she said, "but how did it get that name?"

"You'll see."

So they climbed. It was a gentle, winding ascent, and Carol didn't mind. The forest had enchanted her, and she wondered that she had ever, even in the darkness of night, felt it to be foreboding.

They had been climbing for perhaps an hour when the forest ended. It wasn't that the trees began to thin or taper out; they simply ceased, a ring of stones marking their limit. The ground became rocky and barren, and the path cut through terrain that was utterly devoid of life as it ascended to the crest of the hill, now visible to them.

"What the hell..." Amy mumbled.

"Crazy, right?"

"What happened?" Carol asked as Maggie stepped over the stone circle and continued along the path. The others followed her, albeit with some reluctance.

"Nobody really knows, to be honest with you. It's just always been this way, since the first Europeans showed up in Maine. They guess the Indians did it, though all the local tribes hated the place. So maybe somebody who came before? It's our own little mystery. Anyway, they still don't know what they did to the soil, but nothing will grow here. Not beyond the stones."

"That's *wild*."

"Just wait till you get to the top."

The air had shifted, and Carol's mood with it. What had been a relaxing jaunt through the forest had changed once they reached the hilltop. The day had not been warm, but now it had turned downright cold, and Carol pulled her coat tight around her body. She found herself gasping for breath. The hill was not all that steep, and Carol was in reasonably good shape, but every step was harder than the last to take. By the time they reached the summit, she was exhausted.

What she saw took her remaining breath away.

In any other setting, it would have been the view that she found stunning. Bald Mountain was the tallest of the foothills all the way to the horizon, and from their perch the three women could gaze out upon the entirety of the lake and the forested valleys and rises surrounding it. But it was not nature that drew her eye; it was the great, rough-hewn circle of stone that crowned the hill which held them in its grasp.

"Ta-da!" Maggie said, smiling. Amy and Carol did not react. "Isn't it amazing?" She prodded. "I found it when I was a kid."

"It's amazing," Amy whispered.

Maggie moved within the circle of stone and the other women followed.

"How come I've never heard of this?" said Carol. Maggie shrugged.

"A couple of kids came up with their professor from U Maine to study it once. Nothing ever came of it, I guess. There are these stone rings on hilltops all over New England."

Carol ran her hand down one of the rock pillars. It was cold, so very cold. In the center of the circle was another stone, one that lay on its side and formed a kind of table. There was a deep groove cut into the surface at one end, and Carol wondered what kind of tool possessed by the primitive people who built this megalith could have made that indentation. Beyond the groove was a large hole drilled down into the rock. Carol might have wondered what this was for, but the answer was in the fallen headpiece that lay in the dirt beside the slab—the stone dowel protruding from its bottom would no doubt slide perfectly into the hole.

"Let's take a picture," Maggie said. Whether through familiarity or something else, the dead earth and ancient cairn did nothing to unsettle her. Not as it had Amy and Carol.

"A picture?" Amy said. "How are we going to do that?"

"Carol, you've got your phone?"

"Well yeah, but it doesn't work out here."

Maggie rolled her eyes. "I don't want to make a call. I want to use the camera."

"You got a selfie stick hidden on you somewhere I can't see?"

"We'll sit on that big rock, loser."

"There's nowhere to put it." Amy said. Carol and Maggie looked around, but Amy was right; there was nowhere that made sense. The slab was too low, and the tops of the rock pylons would have been too high, even if they could reach them.

"A piece broke off. If we put it back, we could set the phone on there."

The words hadn't left her mouth before Carol regretted it, but she could not fathom why.

"Do you think we can lift it?" said Amy, eyeing the square of chiseled granite.

"Only one way to find out." Maggie marched over to where Carol stood and nodded to the rock. She squatted down on her haunches, grabbing the dowel with one hand. Then she looked at Carol with expectant eyes. "You gonna help?"

Carol bent over and slid her hands under the stone. She nodded at Maggie and tried to remember to lift with her legs. With two of them and Amy supervising, the stone was surprisingly light.

They maneuvered it over to the slab and tilted it so the dowel slid into the hole. The stone came to rest with an unexpectedly pleasing thump.

"See, nothing to it."

Carol rubbed the back of the stone with the tips of her fingers. There was something there. An indentation, a carving of sorts. The sun was two hours past its meridian. Even through five thousand years of erosion and detritus, the symbol seemed almost to shimmer in the afternoon sunlight. It was a perfect circle, marred only by a single point at its bottom. In the center were three spheres fused together, like the nucleus of an atom in a textbook.

"Hey, spaz," Maggie said, and Carol realized that she and Amy were staring at her. "Set up the camera and let's go. I'm ready to eat!"

Carol placed the phone carefully on top of the ancient stone. She set it for ten seconds and then ran to join her friends. They all smiled and the phone flashed—pointlessly—and the deed was done.

Maggie jogged over and grabbed up the phone. "Perfect!" she declared. Amy seemed equally pleased. Only Carol felt uneasy. Something about the image didn't sit well with her.

A sudden breeze blew the dust in swirling patterns. They gathered up their things and began their descent.

*　*　*

That night was early and uneventful. The women were tired from the walk, and more drinking and smoking did not interest them. Amy made dinner—Amy always cooked—and after spaghetti and meatballs, they all went to bed. Carol's dreams were fevered, filled with dark shadows and creeping things she could not quite see. When she woke, Maggie was downstairs, sitting on the back porch, smoking a cigarette.

"I thought you quit," Carol said. Maggie waved her off.

"I don't make it a habit," she said. "I had some crazy-ass dreams last night. Needed to take the edge off."

"Amy didn't make breakfast?"

"Still in her room."

That wasn't like Amy, Carol thought. She was always the early-to-rise type. Carol went back inside and climbed the stairs. Amy's room was at the top of the riser. The door was closed. Carol knocked. There was no answer.

"Amy, you in there?"

Still, nothing. Carol pushed open the door. Amy's bed was empty.

"Hey, Maggie," she called out, jogging down the steps. Maggie was standing in the kitchen, drinking a glass of orange juice.

"Yeah?"

"Amy's not in her room."

Maggie shrugged her shoulders. "Keys are gone. Maybe she went out."

Amy could see the Land Rover from the front window. "Her car's still here."

"Then maybe she went for a walk, or a run, or whatever. I don't know," Maggie said. "Why do you care so much?"

"It's not like her. She doesn't just wander off."

"Carol," Maggie said, the edge in her voice betraying her thoughts, "just relax. This is the safest place in the world. What's the worst that could have happened?"

After another hour, Maggie started to worry, too. They sat in the kitchen, drinking cups of coffee, one eye on the door and another on the clock.

"I'm going to kill her when she gets back," Maggie mumbled.

"I think we have to do something. Something's not right."

"I don't know what to do."

"We've got to call somebody, maybe. The cops or whatever."

"There's no landline here, and I don't get reception. We're getting away from it, remember?"

"Then we've got to go get somebody."

"Amy took the keys."

"Then we walk—"

"Dammit, Carol! It's 9 miles to the nearest house."

Carol slammed her fist so hard against the counter the coffee cups leapt into the air. "We can't just sit here!"

Maggie held up a hand. "Look, look, let's give it a little more time before we freak out, OK? Then, if we don't hear anything, we'll walk."

So they waited. Amy never came back. Carol had bitten her fingernails down to nubs. She tried to rationalize it, tried to tell herself that it was all going to work out, but none of the scenarios she created that ended with Amy walking through the front door made much sense. Carol was pacing across the room, the feeling that they should be doing *something* so overwhelming she could barely stand it. Maggie sat at the kitchen bar, a coffee cup clutched in one hand, looking as if she was utterly exhausted.

"What if she went for a swim, got a cramp and drowned or something?"

"The lake's freezing," Maggie said. "She wouldn't have done that."

"And she didn't take the car. So either she went for a walk in the woods and something happened or somebody came and took her."

"Nobody took her. And there's nothing in the woods that could hurt her."

"Well something happened. I can't wait any longer. I'm going."

Maggie sighed. Carol couldn't take it.

"Why are you acting like this?" she shrieked. "What's wrong with you?" But Carol knew the answer. Maggie was scared, maybe more than she ever had been before. She wasn't used to being so out of control.

"You're overreacting."

Carol looked like she might explode, and Maggie saw it.

"Fuck it. Let's go."

A flash of light and a boom of thunder. The rain began to pour.

Carol cursed under her breath. She drew back the curtain on the front window just in time to see a bolt of lightning crash into the lake. The sound of thunder followed on top of it, and Carol wondered how such a vicious storm could break upon them so suddenly.

"Oh God," she murmured.

"Well, I guess we're not going anywhere now," Maggie said. Carol heard the relief in her voice.

The hours passed, and yet still the storm raged. The thunder shook the cabin, and when the power finally gave out, the lightning was all that lit it. After a while Carol stopped wondering how a storm could last so long, how it could seem to sit over one place in its fury for hours on end. She thought of the hillside, and the stone, and she knew.

By the time night fell hard on the lake, Maggie was drunk. The two of them sat on the floor, their backs against the breakfast bar. It somehow seemed safer that way.

"My grandfather built this place," Maggie said, dangling the bottle of beer between her knees. "His ancestors had owned the land for forever. Bought it for nothing. But nobody would build out here. Not for generations. The Indian legends, you know?" She took a drink. "My granddaddy, he used to say that there were things in the hills that were older than they should be. That this was a place out of time. 'The trees walk,' he'd say. I never really understood what that meant."

Two words left unspoken, but Carol knew what she was thinking.

Until now.

"It's going to be fine, Mags," Carol said. She hadn't called her that since college. Maggie shook her head.

"Granddaddy said that he built this place to change things. To bring order to chaos. 'The wild is theirs,' he would say. And he thought he could push it back. With a little cabin and running water and electric lights. He died thinking he had. But he was wrong." She had started to cry. "I'm scared, Carol."

Carol reached over and hugged her tight, but there was nothing to say. She was scared, too.

Carol wasn't sure when she fell asleep. In her dreams, she was running through the woods. Stumbling really, her feet slipping in the muck. The rain had stopped, and on the wind, she could hear voices.

She was running to the hillside. She had no choice. She had to go. She was a passenger in her own body. She fell to the ground, crawled on her hands and knees, forced herself back to her feet, and then stumbled across the stone circle. The hilltop ahead glowed preternaturally. Dark figures waited. By the time she made it to the top, they were no longer mere silhouettes.

Amy and Maggie were standing on either side of the stone slab, which Carol now understood was an altar. They were both nude. Carol had seen them that way before, but years prior, before age and self-abuse had taken their toll. And yet, Carol knew that these were not her friends. In body, perhaps, but not in mind. She could see that in their eyes.

Maggie gestured to the slab, bidding Carol to take her place upon it.

"Come, my child. Prepare the way."

In one blinding instant, Carol saw the world pass away, saw it blaze in an unnatural flame, as creatures of a shape and size she could not comprehend moved upon it.

Carol awoke. The storm had ceased. The cabin door was open. The air did not stir. Maggie was gone.

Her phone flashed stupidly on the living room table. She grabbed it up, praying for a signal. But there was none. Her battery was dying; that was all. The screen blinked on, still showing the last image it had displayed—the picture of the three of them on top of the hill. The day before it all fell apart.

Carol started to cry, and for one moment she forgot how uneasy the photo made her feel and longed for the moment it was taken. Then she saw it, and her tears were replaced by terror. It was the shadow that covered them, one that should not have been, not with their backs to the setting sun and nothing behind them to cast it. And yet there it was, moving against the light, falling upon them. It had taken Amy and Maggie already, taken them and done something to them that was worse than death. But Carol knew—it was her that it wanted, and it was coming for her soon.

So Carol waited. She waited, clutching a kitchen knife that could not save her. She waited as the voices of her friends called to her from the forest, from the hillside, from among ruins that were ruins no more.

She waited for the dawn, even as she knew it would never come.

The Return of the Witch Queen

Journal of Carter Weston
October 24, 1926

The legends regarding Nyarlathotep have always been of particular interest to me. It was his relationship to mankind that drew me, his antithesis to the Christ figure. For he was also a god who walked among men. But to destroy, not to save. Still, I found hope in that dependency, in that connection to humanity. If it were true that Nyarlathotep somehow needed men to accomplish whatever foul deeds he sought, then men could stand in the breech against him as well, even if we were always outnumbered by those who would do his bidding.

Only a few years ago, I personally witnessed them and their perversity. I was attending a conference on ancient Sumerian religious cults at Louisiana State University, in the city of Baton Rouge. The conference itself was a waste of time and money, but I did not leave empty handed. Not in the slightest. For there was another at the conference, one who did not belong. Yet he was the most important attendee of them all.

We met in the bar of the Bellemont hotel. He wore a seersucker suit and white patent-leather shoes. But it wasn't his clothes that drew me to him. It was the fact he was reading my second book, *Witch-cults of the Ancient World*. Still, I probably would have let him be, not wanting to draw attention to myself or waste either of our time. But it was not up to me, for he sought me out.

"Dr. Weston," he said, extending his hand. "I had hoped you'd turn up here. I am Inspector John Dubois, up from New Orleans for the conference. Two Sazeracs," he said to the bartender. The man nodded and went to work. Dubois had an easy smile and an innate charm, the kind that made you trust him immediately. I had a sudden feeling that he was very good at extracting confessions. The bartender returned with two glasses of a frothy white liquid I did not recognize.

"To freedom." He took a sip and then held a finger in the air. "I was hoping you would sign this," he said, sliding the book in my direction. As I did, I asked him what would bring a New Orleans inspector of the police to such a conference.

"Interesting you should ask, Professor, for that reason sits before me." Dubois must have seen a hesitancy flash in my eyes, because he put a hand on my arm and laughed. "Oh, it's nothing you've done, Professor. Nothing at all. In fact, it's something I wanted to do *for* you." It was then he began to relay to me the story of many of the strange things he had seen on the job in Orleans Parish. It seemed that one of the cults I had written about in my book—ancient, yes, but certainly not dead—had found its way to the Crescent City.

"Fifteen years or so ago, when I was fresh on the force, we broke up one of their meetings out in the swamps, some thirty miles from the city. Middle of nowhere, kind of place that honest people don't go if they can help it. Arrested a bunch of them, not that we could make the charges stick, even if we did believe that they were involved in some pretty nasty stuff. They left behind an artifact though, one I'm sure you are familiar with. The man in charge of my unit, Inspector Legrasse, spent the rest of his life trying to figure out just what he had."

I was indeed familiar with the artifact. Professor George Angell of Brown University was a dear friend of mine, and he had related to me the very same story that Dubois was now telling. Of how the inspector had discovered an eldritch and untraceable idol—a grotesque, ancient stone statuette—and had sought scholarly advice on the object and the cult that possessed it, much as Dubois was now seeking from me.

"I was under the impression, Inspector, that you had succeeded in driving the cultists out of the city."

Dubois shook his head and scoffed. "Were it so, Professor. New Orleans is not the kind of place that one can purge of such things. Oh, they've gone underground all right, but they are still there. Waiting. That's why I became so interested in your particular area of expertise," he said, gesturing to my book. "Obsessed, my wife says. But when you've seen the things I've seen, you come to believe that men, with the right motivation, are capable of just about anything. And as much as I'd like to believe it weren't so, my eyes don't lie to me."

"So they are active again, you say?"

"They are. It took us a while to get a figure on it. They hide in plain sight, cover their tracks with voodoo and such. The voodoo is harmless enough. Ancestor worship, protective potions, that sort of thing. Mostly hocus-pocus and cheap tricks. But there's one voodooeen who was different, one who had real power."

"Laveau."

He nodded once, throwing back the rest of his drink and ordering another with a nod at the bartender.

"Been dead thirty years at least, but they say she still walks the streets of the Old Quarter, still peddles her wares and her witchcraft. Still preaches her black masses. Sounds crazy, I know. But probably not to you, and certainly not to me."

"And you think there's more to this Laveau woman than voodoo?"

Dubois leaned back against the bar. "Tell me, Professor. What do you know of the Ashmodai?" A grin flashed across his face as a shudder roiled through me. "That's what I thought."

The Ashmodai were, perhaps, the world's first great religion. The fires of their worship had burned through Mesopotamia, down into Africa, and out into the Far East. Their adherents slaughtered men, women, and children by the thousands in Gaul and across the channel in ancient Britain, locking them in towering wooden figures formed in the shape of a man, before burning them to the ground. It is said that the empires of antiquity arose from the maddened cries of savaged peoples, inspired by desperate souls that begged for anyone to save them from the hordes of the Ashmodai. And while the Egyptians and Greeks and Babylonians struck heavy blows against the old faith, it wasn't until the Roman Empire brought the sword and the cross to every known corner of the world that the flame of Asmodeus was extinguished.

And yet, even now, whispers of their continued workings still float across the winds of time, and who can say that they ever truly disappeared?

"Surely," I said, "you don't believe that the Ashmodai have come to New Orleans?"

"You think they *are* dead, then? Truly dead?"

"Dead or not, there's been not one recorded instance of their presence for 1,500 years."

"But there have, haven't there? The nameless cults that exist throughout the world? Maybe not so nameless after all."

It was true that there were those who claimed that the ancient religions had not vanished but simply gone underground, disguising themselves in the garb of more modern faiths. I had seen evidence of such subterfuge, from the Esoteric Order of Dagon, which had spread from New England's own Innsmouth to port cities around the world, to the Circle of the Crescent Moon, which had debased mosques throughout Indonesia.

"Even so," I said, "it seems highly unlikely you would have them in Louisiana, no matter what you've seen."

"Perhaps," he said, staring down into his drink. "Maybe you should come with me to New Orleans, and we can find out together. We think we know where they meet, and I want you there when we break it up."

"Me? But why?"

Dubois was silent, but then he picked up the book that I had signed for him and pointed to it. "Because, Professor. I've read your book, and I've read a lot of others, too. I know more than just about anyone out there about this stuff," he said, gesturing to the hallway where the conference-goers were gathered. "Call it obsession if you want, but I've learned that knowledge is power. And that's why you need to be involved. The Old Ones want chaos, and they thrive on ignorance. If we're going after them in the shadows, then we gotta shine the light of truth on them. That's what you do. 'Cause there can be no faith without seeing truth, and faith is what we need now more than ever."

I didn't need convincing. If even half of what Dubois believed had solid foundation, then the trip to New Orleans was well worth the cost in time and money. In the end, I was not to be disappointed.

* * *

The conference still had a day to go, but I was no longer interested in presentations and scholarly theories. Dubois and I were on the next train to New Orleans, watching the swamps speed by as he relayed what had brought him to Baton Rouge in the first place.

"We found her," he said, "in the cellar of an abandoned tavern on the outskirts of the city. It wasn't a pretty sight, Professor. Not a pretty sight at all. Never seen anything like it. She was split, all the way down her body. Naked, of course. Most of her organs had been taken out and placed around the chamber, some burnt in front of crude altars. To what god, I don't know and don't care to find out. Coroner said she was alive through most of it."

"What do you know about her?"

"Well, nothing, at the time. But we were able to track down a name based on a locket that we found under one of the chairs in the cellar. Probably got ripped off when they were getting her ready. Her name was Janet Barboux, seventeen years old. Her father was a sailor, in and out of New Orleans most times. We've been unable to locate him, but we also can't find a speck of proof that he's aboard any of the ships that have left port in the last month. Sad to say, he's our prime suspect."

"His own daughter?"

The inspector shook his head, but not in denial. "Terrible thing, isn't it? Anyway, once we focused on Barboux, we were able to track down some of his less reputable associates. One of them, a man named Joe—doesn't have a last name that we can find—has a reputation around town as being mentally unstable. Spent some time up at East Louisiana, and they probably should have kept him there. He denied any involvement at first, of course, but we were able to break him. Can't say I'm altogether proud of our methods, but desperate times, right?"

"And what did he say?"

"Claimed he fell into some tough straits. Lost his job, needed money. Someone from his church said they could help. Said they belonged to something special, something that would change his life. They called themselves the *pòt an lò*, creole for the Golden Gate. Things turned for him. He had money in his pocket for the first time in his life. After about a year, they told him the time was right, that the stars had come round. Told him that a sacrifice was needed, the spilling of blood on the death of the moon."

"I assume there was a promise attached to this sacrifice as well?"

"Indeed, there was. If done correctly, the sacrifice opened a doorway on the coming of the next full moon. A gate through which might pass what he called the *bondye wa*, apparently some kind of ancient demon, a messenger of some sort." I must have blanched then, for a shadow of understanding passed over the face of Dubois. "You know of what he speaks? This makes sense to you?"

"I have heard the legends," I mumbled.

"In any event," he said, "the full moon is tonight. With the assistance of this Joe, we were able to track the cult to its heart. A place called La Salle. I'm not surprised. La Salle has quite a reputation, the sort of place that kids make up ghost stories about and old folks shun. It was one of the first permanent settlements in the territory, and would have been the capital, or so they say. The Catholic Diocese built this enormous cathedral in the center of town. Something else to see. But then the floods came. Some people say it was an Indian curse, that the settlers had disturbed old magic better left alone. But whatever the truth, the intentions of the townsfolk, no matter how grand, couldn't stand against the rising waters. Before long, the whole place was a ghost town. It's been that way ever since."

"And that is where we are going?"

"It is. Tonight. My men will meet us at the train station."

We rode in silence then, nothing but the sound of the engine and steel wheels on steel rails to interrupt our thoughts.

*   *   *

The inspector's men were waiting for us at the station, just as he said. There were ten of them, strong men with hard faces that I hoped reflected their hearts. The sun already hung low in the western sky.

"Time is running short," Dubois said, "and we have a ways to travel yet."

We climbed into a couple of pickup trucks. I rode in the cab of one with Dubois, while most of the men settled into their beds, checking and rechecking the rifles they carried.

"You expect a fight?" I asked.

He nodded. "Mmmhm. That's what we got last time. Can't imagine why this would be any different."

Our truck led the way, and we hadn't gone far before we left civilization behind entirely. The swamps and thick woods we had traversed aboard the train did not prepare me for the utter desolation of that world. And yet, even though the green jungle was thick around me, the stench of rotting decay was in the air as well. For this was a dying world, one struck with some disease that went beyond the ordinary realm. Something older. Something more foul.

We rumbled along the broken pavement until the pavement itself ran out. Now it was dirt and rocks, a one-way road that barely deserved the name, a trail that the swamp was gradually swallowing. It seemed that we were no closer to much of anything when we turned off the main path onto an even more perilous lane, but we had not gone far before Dubois pulled behind a copse of trees and killed the engine. "We walk from here," he said, turning to me. "Wouldn't want to give away our approach."

The twelve of us piled out, each man removing a flashlight and switching it on. Dubois addressed his troops briefly, telling them that they had his full faith, his full confidence. They had been with him the longest, and many of them had seen the cult's foul doings in the swamps more than a decade before. Today they would extinguish its flame, once and for all.

"Let's go."

We crept back to the main road, staying in tight formation on either side, ready to dive into the forest at the merest sound of an approaching vehicle. The night was growing thick, and it was only then that I noticed something peculiar. We were in the midst of a great swamp, surrounded by wilderness for a hundred miles, maybe. And yet I heard nothing. Not a bird, not an animal in the brush, not even the insects that normally teem about. No mosquitos feasted upon us. No ancient-eyed owls watched our approach. We were completely alone. It was as if they had foreseen some coming doom that we could only imagine, the maw of which we were now walking directly into.

We'd gone maybe a mile when Dubois held up his hand. "Do you hear that?" We all stopped, craning our necks to try to hear better, to catch some semblance of sound. It started off as a murmur, a thumping echo that I might have mistaken for the beating of my own heart. But it was too regular, even for that. Too deep. That throbbing rhythm, that howling bass. Conga drums, pounding through the night.

"Check your weapons," Dubois whispered. "We'll be upon them any second."

Suddenly the forest changed, and it was only when I peered deep into its depths that I saw why. We were in a town. You would barely know it, since the jungle had claimed it back for nature, but there were buildings in the gloaming of the swamps, covered in vines, long, green arms breaking through that read "Oldman's Apothecary" and "Village Café," all collapsing under the weight of kudzu and Spanish moss. The road was no longer dirt but rather cobblestone.

Dubois gave a signal, and we extinguished our lights. In an instant, we were plunged into a black darkness that swallowed us whole, and I had to fight with all my being not to go running headlong into the wilderness.

The moon was bright that night, though, and the sky clear of obscuring clouds. My eyes soon adjusted and I could see as well as, if not better than, before. We continued on and in no time came to the empty city square, as dead as the end of the world. At the head of that square sat a towering cathedral, made all the more glorious by the vines wreathing it in green. I almost didn't notice the flickering lights within.

Dubois glanced at me before nodding to his men, flicking his hand left and then right. The detectives filed out, forming a rough cordon around the building, surrounding it. They were the hunters. We were the hounds meant to flush our prey. I followed the inspector as he made his way around the old church, searching for some weakness, some point of access. We swung wide of the door; a direct entry would not do. From within, the sound of discordant piping had joined the bestial thump of the drums.

I saw it before Dubois. A ladder, wrought iron, added to the side of the building for easy access, sometime before the cathedral was abandoned forever. I tapped the inspector on the shoulder, disheartened by his startled reaction. If I was looking for a rock on which to lean during this journey, he was not it. I gestured toward the ladder. He followed my eyes, nodding back at me when he saw it.

We began to climb.

I was not entirely convinced that the rust-rotten iron would hold us, but it was our best bet. If I was to fall to my death in the midst of that swamp, so be it.

Our target was an opening high on the cathedral wall, a window meant to provide ventilation and light during happier times. It still might, if we could squeeze through it. I had my doubts about Dubois, raised as he was on the sumptuous fare of Louisiana, but he managed to pass with little effort. I followed him, and we found ourselves inside.

The sound which had been growing with intensity as we climbed boomed through the dank attic of the church. Light seeped through the wooden slats of the floor, illuminating motes of dust that swirled and danced around us. I found myself stifling a sneeze, knowing that such a mistake would spell the end of us both. We crawled forward on our hands and knees, careful not to make a sound, though I wondered if our weight alone was raining down the accumulated dirt and detritus of many decades on the adherents below. Not that they would have noticed in the frenzy of their exultations. We were in luck, in any event, for, not ten feet from us, a great square had been cut in the floor, a skylight through which we could peer without fear of discovery.

We crawled forward, every creak of every beam sending lightning bolts of terror into the pit of my stomach, and yet the sound of drums and pipes and now human voices was enough to drown all sound, if not all fear. There was a smell too, a combination of burning smoke and something sweet I couldn't place.

And then we peered over that edge to below and looked upon madness made flesh.

The cathedral floor was a shambles of all that is holy. Rotten pews and prayer kneelers had been torn up and shoved into piles along the side, save where the boards would serve a purpose. The wood had been fashioned into crude St. Andrew's crosses, though I knew well that this ungodly crew had another name for the implements of death that surrounded the gathered mass in a large semi-circle.

"The mark of the harbinger," I dared to whisper to Dubois. "The sign of the cult of Nyarlathotep."

Would that they had been empty. The people—three men, three women, and worst of all, a boy who could not have been more than seven or eight years old—that hung, spread-eagled, from them were beyond saving. I knew then what the smell was: the scent of rotting flesh, mingled with the smoke from the torches that illuminated the room. Skin hung loose and low from the naked bodies, and in places—especially around the face—it had peeled off. The stench was overwhelming, and I marveled that I hadn't recognized it earlier.

The cultists numbered a couple of dozen. Their god was no respecter of persons. Among their ranks were men and women, young and old, rich and poor, black and white. At their front stood a single figure, her long, black robe decorated with strips of fabric in every color, head wrapped in a crimson scarf that seemed to climb into the sky. A priestess of Nyarlathotep, or so her bearing said, though there was nothing soft or feminine or motherly about her. She was the sword of the god, the bringer of his vengeance, the sower of his destruction. Lying before her on what must have been the cathedral's once-holy altar was a youth, a man of perhaps eighteen. He was nude, and no bindings held him down. He was either there of his own volition or, more likely, drugged for the sacrifice.

Dubois removed his pistol and a whistle from his pocket. Once he gave the signal, his men would rush the building, and in the confusion we hoped to take our prisoners without violence. But if they had weapons, Dubois was prepared to take down anyone who threatened his men. He put the whistle to his lips, but I stopped him with a hand to his shoulder. He looked at me, and without words, he knew I wanted to see more. The woman below began to cast her spell.

When she spoke, I was surprised that her words were not English or French or even Creole. They were much older—Sumerian—an ancient tongue from the ancient people who first wrote of Nyarlathotep, before the Egyptians gave him the name by which we know him best. I record her words here, as closely as I can. The translation, though rough, conveys all the truth of those dread utterances.

Her voice started as a whisper, rising to a murmur, and then soaring to a roar. "Alal. Alla xul. Nisme! Ati me peta babka! Kanpa! Taru! Iksuda! Negeltu xul labiru ensi ersutu!" *Destroyer. Dark god. Hear me! Throw open the gate between worlds! Remember! Return! Conquer! Then shall the old gods awake and restore their dominion over the earth!*

A roar shook the foundations of the old church. It was below, above, and around all at once. The cultish fires flared, and yellow smoke poured from their flickering flames. The sallow fog gathered around the altar. Reaching tentacles probed upwards, wrapping the body of the boy, covering him in a blanket of golden mist. The youth breathed deep, sucking the yellow smoke into his lungs.

And I knew.

"This is no sacrifice," I whispered.

An explosion roared from Dubois's pistol and through the church. A bullet ripped off the back of the youth's skull. Another roar followed quickly, but of a completely different quality. And if I hadn't known better, I would have said that this hate-filled cry erupted from a demonic maw that formed in the midst of the now-dissipating fog.

What followed was chaos. Dubois was firing wildly, as many in the cult had drawn weapons and were shooting toward the ceiling. The front doors of the church burst open, and in poured Dubois's army. With their guns added to his, the battle was short-lived. When it was over, a dozen cultists lay dead, the same number in custody.

The enigmatic woman who had led them had escaped, seemingly vanished into thin air. I had caught her eye, just after Dubois fired his first shot. She gazed up through the portal that framed our faces. And when her eyes met mine, I would swear that a dark smile crept up the corners of her mouth.

Was that the end of the New Orleans coven? Who can say? But I think we had stumbled upon something far more significant than a simple cult, dedicated to some lost and forgotten deity. We had seen something older and more dangerous. This handful of devotees had come within moments of calling forth the dark one himself, the black messenger of Azathoth. And if even they were able to come so close, then what hope do we have of stopping others in the future?

I visited her grave before I left New Orleans, the voodoo queen, Marie Laveau. I left the offering of bourbon and I made the three x's on her tombstone, as so many devotees seeking favor from beyond the veil have done before me.

But my wish was different. My wish was that neither she, nor the dark god she served, would ever return.

Nemesis

I must write quickly. The candle is dying even now and I can hear them waiting, just beyond the circle of the light.

The coming of Nemesis was a cause for celebration. Since men first looked to the sky and understood it, we had wondered if there was a world beyond the ones we know. Something to account for the wobble in Neptune's orbit. An answer to what titanic love affair had left Uranus to roll forever on its side. A Planet X, a Niburu, a Yuggoth. Yet in the end, it was not a planet that haunted the edge of the solar system, but a star. A dark, dead star. Black as the void and almost as hard to see.

It was a chance scan by an infrared camera on Voyager III that found it. The experts, of course, didn't call it by any of the names the ancients had known. To them, it was Tyche, not an enemy to be cursed but a friend to be welcomed. And so, when I taught my 11th grade science class about its coming, I told them they had nothing to fear.

The black dwarf's orbit took it deep into space, far beyond even tiny Pluto, and for thousands of years it remained but a myth. But now it was coming. A great, dark mass in the sky, one that would blot out the stars until, in an event not seen since the plains of Giza were thick with verdant foliage and echoed with rushing streams, Tyche would blot out the sun as well…

And we would celebrate, the world all over. Muslim and Jew, Christian and Atheist, every race and every people, united by an event so stupendous, so rare, that it might never come again. Not, at least, while mankind still exercised dominion over the earth.

Scientists couldn't even say how long this before-unimagined eclipse would last. Only that it would cover the sun completely for at least a few hours, maybe as long as a day.

And so events were planned. Twilight festivals to embrace the coming dark. We walked into that stygian night with arms wide open. We came to embrace the void. We did not fear the dark, not this time, not anymore.

What madness took hold of us? What fiendish power corrupted our minds? I suppose we will never know, though I have my suppositions. I will always believe that that black orb cast down more than darkness on the surface of the earth, even before *they* came.

Were there some who dissented? I'm sure there were many. But there was only one in our town. One man who did not fall under Tyche's sway. Only one who called what was coming by its own name.

I knew Bill Atwood for nearly a decade. That he taught astronomy and physics at the local college belied his immense stature in the world of academia. At least, the stature he had once maintained. Before he came to our little town in the shadow of the Rockies, he had been a professor of some renown at a prestigious school back East. A scandal had led to his fall from grace and departure from Massachusetts, something about bizarre and controversial views that did not comport with the standard model of the universe or the accepted story of human history, views that he was not shy about sharing. I had heard the end came when his obsession turned to violence and he assaulted the Dean of Sciences at his former employer. That incident had led to his journey west, led him to a place where a struggling college was willing to look the other way in order to hire a man of his expertise. And yet, despite his reputation, I had never personally heard Professor Atwood express any unorthodox views. Not until the coming of Nemesis.

For that is its name, Nemesis. Atwood told me as much. Atwood knew the truth. If only we had listened. But what difference would it have made? Who can stand in the face of such darkness?

I saw him that day, the last day I guess anyone saw him. He was coming out of the grocery store, his cart loaded down with canned food, bottled water, candles. These weren't supplies for holding a celebration, but for surviving a siege.

"Bill?" I said, and I was unable to mask the concern in my voice. When he looked up at me, in his eyes I saw a desperate man. He grasped my arm.

"Howard," he said. He was agitated. Nervous. Afraid. But more than that. He was terrified. "You've always been kind to me. Now I'm going to return the favor. Get out while you can. Find a place to hide."

"Professor," I said, "I'm afraid I don't understand. The festival..."

"This is no time to celebrate!" he almost screamed. I glanced around nervously to see if others were watching. They were, and without approval. "Don't you understand? It's all been written. It's all been predicted. *They* are coming. I tried to warn the others, but they wouldn't listen. Not that it matters..." His speech trailed off, his eyes following. "There's nothing that can stop them. Not then. And not now.

"I have a storm shelter," he said, looking back up at me. "It's not much, but it might be enough. You can come with me. There is plenty of room."

"Thank you, but that's alright, Professor," I said, trying to humor him. Trying to be kind. He reached into his basket and pulled out a votive candle. "Take it," he said. "A guard against the night."

"No, Professor, I can't..."

"Take it! In the end it probably won't matter. But maybe it will buy you enough time." He gestured at me with the glass-encased candle, and this time I didn't protest. He nodded to me once more, and then he was gone, leaving me standing at the entrance of the Save 'n Shop, candle in hand.

I write by that candle now, though I know not for how much longer it will last. Just as I do not know for how long the darkness will hold sway. Too long, no doubt.

The day of the festival was as clear and bright as any I could remember. A perfect blue sky spread above us, unblemished, but for the dark circle of night that seemed to grow larger with every second.

It rolled through the void toward us, blocking out the sky with its great, dark mass. I stood at the base of College Hill while many more waited on its crown, staring up at that coming darkness.

"It's so awesome!" a little boy squealed.

"Yeah, it sure is," a man, his father I assumed, said in answer, cheerfully. And yet, the smallest doubt had crept into his voice. I felt it, too. For the first time, I wondered. But still I stood there, gazing up into the circle of night that slowly devoured the sky.

It was noon when it reached the sun, which sat upon its throne at the apex of the blue dome above us, bathing us in its light as it had since when the earth was devoid of life. We gazed up as the edge of that flat circle of light clashed with the darkness of another. We watched as that greater darkness covered the lesser light. Watched as the sun vanished behind an impenetrable shroud.

A shadow fell over us all. It crept over the town, fingers of night wrapping around homes and stores and schools. It marched up the hill, gaining strength as our star's power diminished. I stared at the sun, a fading disk that no doubt seared the edge of my retina. But I could not look away, any more than a man can look away as the love of his life drives off into the distance, never to be seen again.

I had to experience this, even if I didn't understand. I had to watch, even if I didn't see. I had to bear witness as the first chapter of Genesis was undone. As the second darkness fell upon the surface of the earth. As God said, "Let there be night." But not God. Something else. Something else entirely.

The end began with a sound. Though that's not really the right word. It was more like a buzzing, something that was felt more than heard. A low, inaudible murmur, just beyond the range of man's hearing.

But then there was something that we did hear. A cry, a wail, a piteous howling, more desperate than any I'd ever heard before. It was the dogs, you see. It was as if every dog in town was suddenly struck by such pain or sorrow that they could not bear it but by calling out to the world in the only way they knew how.

The sound unsettled the children. It unsettled the adults, too, but they tried to keep a brave face. Reassurances were given. Soothing words spoken that, to my ears at least, lacked conviction.

It was after the howl of the dogs had ceased that we first saw it. The night was dark, and Nemesis was darker. And yet as that black mass hung in the sky, I began to believe that I could make out something curling off of the dead star's surface. Smoke-like tendrils seemed to reach toward us. Tentacles of swirling mist drifted down from the beyond and spread across the sky. The noonday stars that had seemingly winked into existence as the sun's rays faded were extinguished. And then something even stranger happened. The lights of the city—the street lamps, the storefronts, even the white Christmas bulbs that decorated the stage on College Hill—began to flicker and fade until, one by one, they all went out. The darkness that had covered the sky now covered the earth.

Panic was in the air. The voice of the crowd gibbered and murmured as fear spread through us all. And yet still we clung to the belief that this was nothing unusual, and that even if it was, it too would pass in good time. That belief was broken when we heard the first scream.

It seemed to fall down from the summit above to those of us who could get no closer than the base of College Hill. It was on that summit that the breath of Nemesis now alighted, where, as impossible as it seemed, the shimmering tendrils of darkness that drifted down from it now touched. I suppose when we heard the first cry that it should have snapped nerves already on edge, should have sent us screaming into the night. Instead it froze us in place and caused all of us to glance toward our neighbors for assurances, even as they were hidden from our view.

It was a scream like a whistle on a freight train passing through a town at rush hour. It never really stopped, only took a breath to reload. It seemed to grow closer, and as my eyes adjusted to the darkness I saw a man running toward us. He was the one screaming. The sound of it curved along the Doppler Effect as he ran to me and past me, his wail carrying into the night. Then there was movement. You could sense it as much as see it. The crowd at the top of the hill was frothing, bulging and contracting, pushing against itself, spilling down the slope.

What was one scream became a thousand.

The people around me began to run, picking up their children and going. But in the darkness they could not see. Many fell, never to rise again, crushed beneath the boots and heels and tennis shoes of their neighbors. I could not move, paralyzed by fear and wonder and even curiosity. I stood there as the wave of terrified men and women and children broke around me, surging down the hill and into town, fleeing without direction or thought, knowing, like a herd of hunted prey, that they must escape, must get away. I don't know why I stayed. Perhaps because I sensed that something was coming, something I needed to see.

And see it I did, though I can't say even now exactly what it was. At first I saw only the carnage it wrought, as one might look upon a tree snapped by the wind. Bodies were ripped asunder before me, torn or sliced or twisted apart as if by impossibly powerful and unseen hands. I staggered back, until finally I was sprinting full speed after those who'd gone before.

It was only when I chanced a glance over a shoulder that I saw one, and only then in the corner of my eye (I wonder now if we can see them otherwise, if perhaps to look upon them fully would break something in the mind). It was madness made reality, shadow given form, something made of nothing.

A thing that walked when it should have crawled.

How to describe what shouldn't exist in a sane world? Even to try is to struggle against our rational boundaries. It was a creature made of sharp and impossible angles, a being of form unknown to man even in the worst nightmares of the insane. I watched as its scythe-like arms sliced through body and bone, as its titanic empty maw devoured the living and the dead. And it was not just one. It was legion.

I ran on, but there was no escaping the things that came from the sky, no escaping Nemesis as it poured out its hate.

I fled as my friends and neighbors were consumed by a dark fire that covered all. Somehow I found my way, stumbling through empty alleys and naked corridors, back here, to my home, to my study, to what may be the final source of light in all the world. The flickering flame of a candle, all that's left to hold back the night.

I know my time is short. As I've written this, the shrieks and screams and pleas for help and mercy that filled the streets beyond my door have fallen silent. And now they have come for me. They wait, just beyond the circle of the light, swirling, snarling, hating. Thirsting for my blood, my pain, my death. They creep forward as the light retreats, and my candle is all but gone. I will write until I can write no more. I hope that others survived this. I pray that someone will live to see a new day, that they will find this testament of one who did not believe.

But if not, then if some other creature should come upon it and decipher the meaning of it, they will know that not all stars give life, and that not all life is meant to walk within the light.

The candle flutters. I can sense them now. Hear them. I can feel their claws upon my back, taste the hate upon their breath, hear their frenzy for my doom.

The light is fai

The Spaces Between Space

I must tell you, gentlemen. Before we begin I want to be perfectly clear. I have no memory of how I came to be in the particle accelerator beneath the College, or whose blood it is that stains my clothes. Whether it's Dr. Oxford's, and where his body has gone if it is. I know only two things—Dr. Oxford is dead. And even the darkest of beings longs to return home.

Dr. Oxford and I were friends, this is true. But I had not spoken with him in the better part of five years. I see your interested glances, but I can assure you that there were no ill feelings between us. It was simply that work had consumed both of our lives, and we had no time for friendships, no matter how good they may have once been.

You ask me what happened to Dr. Oxford. You question me as if I should know. Given the circumstances I suppose that is not surprising. In truth, I do not know what happened that accursed night. But I know what I believe. And that, my friends, I will reveal to you now, though I am under no illusions. When you hear my story, you will likely think me mad. Oh, were it so! The madman has the comfort of living in a world of illusion. He need not fear the shadow, the thing that moves in the darkness. That fills the spaces between space. Lurking in the abyss and the void, in the dark places between the stars. No, to be mad would be comfort.

If you are to know what took Dr. Oxford, then you must first know what he believed. Oh yes, I am sure you are aware of his reputation. I know that your research has told you many things. That Oxford was renowned in the field of astrophysics. That he had been asked to lead the Large Hadron Collider project and had accepted. That he was respected in all corners of science and that his theories were as praised as they are now mainstream. That is the Dr. Oxford that you know. It is not the one I knew. It is not the face that he revealed to his closest friends.

No, Oxford believed *other* things.

I suppose you have heard of what some call dark matter. No? Well, maybe that is not too surprising. I don't want to bore you, gentlemen, so I'll keep it short. The universe as we know it functions in a specific way. A regular way, a predictable way. It is because of that regularity that we can do things that generations before would have seen as no less than magic. Ah, but there is a problem with our theories. We know *how* the universe works, but we don't know *why*. The fact is, there's not enough of the everyday material in our familiar world to make it function as it does. That leaves us with only one conclusion. There must be something else. Something unusual, exotic. Something that we do not understand. We call that something dark matter. That is what fills those spaces between space. You see, the light could not be without the darkness. And reality as we know it could not be if the darkness ceased to exist.

Most of my colleagues leave it there. This dark matter simply *is*, somewhere, somehow. It makes the planets move about the sun and the sun turn round the center of the galaxy and that is that. But Dr. Oxford had a theory.

Ordinary matter, in what form does it exist? You see it every day. It is the rocks and the trees, the dirt beneath your feet and the air that you breathe. It is the sun that shines in the sky and the planets that whirl around it. It is the cock that crows in the morning, and the birds that sing at night. It is you and it is me.

Dr. Oxford simply asked the obvious question. If ordinary matter does not exist in some undifferentiated mass, why should dark matter?

I can see that even you recognize the implications of that suggestion. Another universe, not one theoretical or hypothetical, not some alternate dimension better suited for fiction than reality.

No, one here, just beyond our vision, hiding in the darkness. And why not? Why not dark stars and dark worlds? Why not...dark life?

Your skepticism does not surprise me. Man sees the world and he believes that what he sees is all that can be. And if you had told someone five hundred years ago that on every surface live millions of beings, so small the eye cannot see them, he would have called you mad. And yet today we accept that simple truth without question. And why? Because now we can see it, of course. And once we see, we believe. We are all like Thomas of old—ever doubting. Dr. Oxford knew that others would react just as you have. That they would laugh at him. That he would lose all that he had built, all that he had created.

And so he decided to help them see.

That is why he took the position with the LHC. During the day, he followed the program's specifications, performing the experiments as they were laid out. Searching for certain particles that are important to science but matter not one whit to the rest of the world. But at night he pursued his true goal. Then he sought a breakthrough that would change the way we view not only ourselves, not only our world, but everything that is. He sought to see what is beyond. To see the substance of shadow. And gentlemen, I tell you now, I believe he did see.

He called me yesterday, three days after the massacre. I had seen the news. How could one miss it? The heart of the Collider itself had been smashed. Six scientists were found slain in the control room. I knew most of them. They had been handpicked by Oxford, his true believers. But Oxford was not among them; he had disappeared completely.

Details were scarce at first. We knew that they had died but not how. Then the rumors started. Wild. Fantastic. Insane. As rumors often are, more diabolical with every telling. But what scared me the most was that I knew there must be truth there. A kernel of fact. And if even part of what people said was true, then it was too horrible to imagine. Bodies ripped to shreds, some so mangled that they could only be identified by the badges they wore.

The police said Oxford had gone crazy. That he had murdered his six colleagues. In a way, that would almost be comforting to believe. But how could you? Forget that Oxford was my friend. Forget that I could never believe him capable of murder. Look at the facts; it was a physical impossibility. How could one man, not frail but old nonetheless, kill six young and healthy men and women? How could he even begin to do the things that were claimed? To literally obliterate the bodies? To turn them into pulp and blood and bone. No, it could not be him. And that was the worst thought of all. Then I received the phone call.

It was Oxford, and there was fear in his voice. He had come to Boston, but how he had gotten to this city was a mystery to me. I knew that the authorities were looking for him. There was no way he could have boarded an international flight without being detected. But he was here, and he wanted to meet. It was that palpable fear that seemed to drip off of every word that convinced me. I suggested several places, but he accepted none.

"It must be a sunny place," he said. "Bright. Full of light."

We chose the Common. We would meet there at noon, when the sun was highest in the sky. I arrived early and waited. When I saw him, my first thought was joy. Relief. Happiness that he had survived. That he was really there. But I could not hold those feelings long. Oxford had seen something. And that cyclopean terror had shattered him, sapping the strength that remained in his body. It had made his eyes wild and fearful, and had drained the vibrancy from his cheeks and the color from his hair. He grasped my hand and I could feel him shaking, shivering as if it were the bitterest day he had ever known.

"James," he said, "thank God you came."

I did not know where to begin or what questions to ask. There were so many.

"Dr. Oxford," I said, "everyone is looking for you. We thought you might be dead."

"I believe I may be, though I can't be sure."

"What?" I whispered. Whatever horror he had witnessed that awful night in the depths of the facility, it had broken his mind. "Dr. Oxford, we must get you to the authorities. And then to a hospital."

"No, James. The authorities would never believe me, and I fear I am beyond any help the hospital might provide. I do not know why it spared my life."

"*It?*"

"I was right, James. I was right. God curse me I was right. We had been running experiments nightly, attempting to probe the dark matter in whatever form or shape it might take. Three nights ago we had a breakthrough. Three nights ago, we saw... We saw."

"What did you see?"

By now Dr. Oxford was shaking so terribly that I feared he could not stand. In his eyes I saw him relive that night, and I thought he might break from it.

"It cannot be described," he said. "It cannot. Only seen. But pray God you never see it."

"But Dr. Oxford, I don't understand. Why are you here?"

"It brought me here, James. It wants something, but its mind is too vast. It's too vast and I cannot know what it seeks! But it fears the light. It fears the light as darkness must and I was able to escape. But it will find me again. It will find me."

To that point the strong, noon-day sun had shone down upon us. But as Dr. Oxford spoke a wind began to blow, and it drew forth clouds. Steel-gray clouds. Dark and ominous clouds. And then I felt as much as saw a shadow fall upon us. Dr. Oxford's eyes went wide. His mouth began to shake. He reached out and grabbed my arm and I knew that if I were not there he would no longer be standing.

But he was not looking at me. No. His gaze was just beyond my shoulder. I felt...cold. And then the hairs raised on my neck and I knew. Whatever had haunted Oxford stood behind me then. In my mind I thought I could feel its breath, cold and full of hatred. And in the corner of my eye I even saw it, though I did not have the courage to turn and look full upon it. Instead, I saw only the form of it. The nebulous blackness, the pulsating, glowing darkness. The bulbous shadow. The being that will plague my night-haunted dreams until this life should end.

You ask me what happened then? Were that I could say, gentlemen. I found myself as you found me. Standing beneath the

College in my laboratory. The particle accelerator running in a configuration I had never used. Whirling and churning. Set into motion not by my hands. And then there was the blood, the blood that covered all.

You'll never find Oxford. And you'll never find his killer. For whatever killed Oxford is the very thing that took us to my laboratory. That used me to gain entrance and Oxford to set the parameters for the accelerator, just as he had before. Whatever dark eminence surrounded us, it is gone now.

Gone home.

The Substance of Shadow

They tell me that space didn't always drive men mad. But I find that hard to believe. I suppose if all you ever did was float around the Earth, go to the moon, take a walk in the void, then space is an adventure. But it's not like that anymore. Not out here.

"This can't be right."

David is talking to himself. He keeps looking at the same coordinates. I know he isn't talking to me, so I just let him repeat it over and over again. "This can't be right."

They say that the problems began when they started going farther. To Mars. Venus. Beyond. It was Earth, you see. People were fine when they could see Earth. When it was just beyond them. Like they could reach out and touch it. But when it was no more than a great, big, blue star…when it was gone, truly gone, irrevocably gone…then they would break. And it's a dangerous thing, that. Nothing worse than a mad man when you are oh so very far from home.

I had woken David from his cryo-sleep. The message came through at 22:30 hours Earth-time. It sounded like words, but none I could understand. I traced the origin of the signal to a blank part of space a half day from our location. Just a dark and empty spot. Nothing there.

Not at first.

"You'd better wake Captain Alexi."

I've thought I was losing it before. On the interstellar flights. When it's not just the Earth but the sun itself that dims into blackness and the void. Those flights only take a few weeks now, since they invented the FTL drives. I remember when I was a kid, they said that was impossible. That our physics wouldn't allow it. So we found new physics to fit our dreams. So now we do it all the time. Flip a switch, watch the Earth and Jupiter and Neptune disappear behind you. And then it's just you. Just you and some points of light to keep you warm. But they give no warmth.

One story has always stuck with me. One story I never forgot. The space jockeys talk about it, or whisper about it, at least. Some say it was the *Chronos*, others the *Excelsius* or the *Kobiyashi*. I don't guess it matters. But they all agree that the ship left Earth with a crew of three men, just like our ship. Two were in cryo-sleep. Just like our ship. But something went wrong. The one who stayed awake, somewhere out there in that endless night, he saw something. Something so terrible, so terrifying that he couldn't go on. Some say he killed himself. Others just say he snapped. That he walked into the crew's quarters, overrode the computer and went to sleep. And so the *Chronos* never reached its destination. Instead it sails on through the void. For hundreds of years it will continue, until the ship has gone so far that it leaves our very galaxy. Until even the Milky Way is just a pin-prick of light in the distance. But one day the crew of the *Chronos* will awaken. Thousands of light years from home. Never to return. Lost in pure, unflinching darkness.

I tap the screen and bring up the computer's cryo controls. I slide the image of a tab upward and click yes to confirm. Captain Alexi will be awake in thirty minutes. Which is plenty of time. The ship—the one that wasn't there before, the one that seems to have appeared from nothing—won't intersect with us for another few hours.

Ships disappear sometimes. Just vanish. They shouldn't, of course. Not today. Not with our technology. You should always be able to find *something*. A beacon. A signal. Debris. That's what we like to tell ourselves. We like to say that if something happens, the rest of the world will know. We won't just be lost. We won't just disappear. Unknown but not forgotten, with families left behind that don't know whether to hope or to cry.

And you see things. In the darkness. You look out into the void where there shouldn't be anything. Nothing but emptiness. And you stare. You stare until the black hole seems to be a thing unto itself. Then you see it. In the corner of your eye, in the shadow beyond. A shimmer, a ripple. Where space seems to curve and turn. Twisting and writhing. And you see it but you say you don't. That it cannot be. But you saw it. You did. You know the truth.

And that's why some ships never come back.

Captain Alexi walks onto the bridge and pulls on his jacket. "What's this about?"

He is stern but not angry. He's scared and I see it in his eyes but he is trying to hide it. He knows that we would never wake him unless something was wrong.

"Jake received this transmission three hours ago."

David flips a switch.

The sound starts to play from the speakers above us and we all look up as if looking up will help us hear it better. It crackles and scratches for a second. Then the static breaks and the sounds are no longer formless and without purpose. We all hear words. But we all tell ourselves that we don't. I look at the other two and watch them. I see that same flicker of understanding I had, when the transmission first came through.

I hear seven words. And so do they. Those words are followed by the sound of rending metal. Then, nothing.

"Can't make it out," Alexi says. "Pull up the ship's course."

I look over at David. His face is white but he just nods. I tap a couple commands and the course of the ship is displayed on the screen, from where it is to where it was when our computer first got a reading off of it. It leads back to that empty bit of space. No farther.

"Pull up the rest."

"That's it, sir."

He looks at me and I think he's angry. Another mask.

"What do you mean that's it?"

"When the message first came in," I say, "I triangulated the signal. I got this quadrant of space. It's empty. Blank. There was nothing. Not a planet, not a moon, not a ship for three days' journey. So I ran a diagnostic. But before it could finish I looked up and…well, there it was."

"The ship?"

"The ship."

Alexi leans over, spreading his arms wide across the console and staring hard at the image below, as if through concentration an answer will present itself. I watch a bead of sweat crawl down his cheek, and I know what he is thinking.

"What are our options, Mr. Sykes?"

David swallows hard and says, "Well sir, obviously under the laws of salvage she is ours if she's derelict. But we aren't required to act, of course. Only if there are lives in danger and we can do so without putting ourselves at risk. And there is no evidence that anyone is still on that ship."

I watch Captain Alexi jerk his head up and look at David. He knows the truth as well as I do, and even if Alexi wants to believe the lie, he can't do it with a good conscience. So instead he points to the screen and says, "Jake, are we close enough for a scan?"

"Yes, sir," I say. "I ran one as soon as we were in range. The hull is intact. No signs of damage. But none of life either."

"Well, we know how accurate those scans can be."

Not very, I think to myself. But good enough for an excuse when one is needed. But Alexi is determined.

"We will intersect her in four hours. Jake, Mr. Sykes and I will go aboard. You will stay on the ship and monitor our progress. I have a feeling we won't find anything, and it will be a nice salvage award for us all."

I look up at David and I see nothing but terror in his eyes.

* * *

The ship is still thirty minutes away when I can first make it out through the visual scanners. It's a freighter, only slightly bigger than ours. It's probably crewed by three men at the most. It could be carrying any manner of cargo. Just another ship. Nothing to make it any different from all the others that ply the void. Or at least that's what I tell myself.

The comm flashes and I tap a button. The screen changes to the airlock. Alexi and David are both in their flight suits.

"Bringing her in now, sir," I say.

The computer does most of the work, setting us up perfectly so that the universal locks can align themselves. The ship shudders and I with it. We are connected. Alexi and David pull down their masks just in case there was a decompression that is not reading on the scan. As they do, the screens to my left and right flicker. One is now David's view. The other, Alexi's. I watch through their eyes as the air lock door spins and then opens. A mechanical arm retracts the door of the other ship and the two men step through the portal. I am alone. I pray they are the same.

Alexi's voice crackles over the comm.

"Air lock intact. No sign it's been used. Accessing the computer." His hand moves up into the screen and I see him tap a few times on the panel. Nothing happens. "Power seems to be out. We got no lights in here other than our own. Computer isn't working. If the doors won't open, then this will be a short trip."

He reaches in front of him and pulls the manual release on the main door. It slides clear in a rush and a crash. The boom echoes into the black maw that opens up before them. Then silence.

"Looks like the power to the doors still works. We are going in."

Alexi's light pierces through the blackness and reveals nothing but a bulkhead beyond. David follows him. Very closely.

"We'll head to the bridge. Should be able to find out what happened there."

They turn down a main hallway. I watch as they walk past darkened corridors that run off in any direction, and I feel my eyes deceive me as I see movement beyond, the illusion of what cannot be. Only the sound of their breathing can be heard. That and the thudding of footsteps, the sound of which I tell myself is only of two men, not more.

And then they came to the door to the bridge.

To that point, nothing had been wrong. Nothing was amiss. But the door. That door! They should have turned back then. I would have told them so, if I had the words to speak. But the only sound was of Captain Alexi unclasping his side arm.

There was nothing extraordinary about the door itself. No, it looked exactly like the one that led to our bridge. But something had happened. I barely know how to describe it. It all seems so fantastic. But in the center were five lines. Five jagged lines, running parallel together like lightning bolts from right to left.

Alexi put his hand up to the door. He removed his glove and ran his fingers down those horrible indentations. And as he did my mind stretched for excuses. For something to explain those five lines dug into titanium. When I saw Alexi raise his weapon, nothing ever seemed so impotent a gesture. Then he pulled on a lever and the door slid to the side.

The lights of both men flooded the room beyond. And as they did my mind played a dozen tricks on me, and I saw things that would have sent me screaming into the night if I had been on that ship. But then the room cleared and there was nothing. Just some blank display screens and empty chairs. The two men moved inside. Captain Alexi walked to the computer and removed a portable power supply he had carried from the ship. He plugged into the console. The screen flickered once and died. Then it sprung to life. The captain keyed in an emergency code and the ships logs came up. No emergency life pods had been deployed. No damage was detected. Then the face of a woman met us; the captain.

There was nothing unusual. She was smiling. She explained the nature of the trip. They were transporting T-97 terraforming units. And that's when I felt my blood run cold. I saw David and Alexi look at each other, and they knew the same thing I did. Alexi reached down and pushed a button. The date of the entry came up. Fifteen years. It had been made over fifteen years before. The T-97 had been obsolete for the better part of a decade.

I could hear Alexi's breath like waves pounding against the rocks. He punched the computer ten times, past log after log until finally he reached the last one. Until finally he would have the answer. But nothing. Just another smiling face. Another peaceful day. Nothing out of the ordinary. Nothing strange.

"That can't be," he said, and I heard panic there. "There has to be something. There has to be an answer!"

There was a sound. Both men froze. I can't describe it, and I doubt they could either. It was like a scratch, but not. Not smooth enough. No, it was like an echo of an echo. A yawning, stretching screech. But in truth, it didn't matter what it sounded like. It was a sound where none should be, and that was enough.

"Oh God, what was that?" It was David, and he was scared.

"Shhh!" Alexi commanded.

My eyes went back and forth between the two screens while the two men looked around the room, trying to find the sound. Alexi stopped.

"Wait. What…" he began, but his words failed him. I stared at what he stared at. I stared but I did not see. "What…" he tried again. Then, in the corner of his eye, in the corner of mine, I saw movement. I saw the shimmer. He turned to look at it, and both screens went black.

I sat there, staring at nothing but white snow. I clicked the comm button. I called, I begged, I pleaded. "Come back!" I screamed. "Captain! David! Anybody!"

And then I wished that they hadn't heard.

One television came on, Captain Alexi's, though I couldn't tell what was going on. It was like the screen was swinging back and forth. I felt the urge to vomit, and it took all I had to contain it. And then I realized what I was seeing. Captain Alexi was running. Down the main corridor, closer and closer to the air lock. Closer and closer to escape.

"Captain! Captain, what's going on!"

He didn't really answer me, and I realized only then that he had been talking the whole time. Talking, screaming, gibbering. Talking to no one. Talking to everyone. In words I couldn't understand. I heard him mention God. I heard him ask for forgiveness. I heard him mention my name. And then he stumbled and the screen went blank again.

"Captain!" I cried. And then I heard. I heard and I didn't hesitate before I turned to the computer and disconnected the airlock. Before I swung the vessel around and engaged the engines. Did it surprise me that there was no longer a ship on my screen? That the computer registered nothing but blackness and void? No, no it didn't surprise me at all. And I have never regretted what I did that day.

Oh yes, I heard.

The captain's screen went dead. But his comm didn't. No, his comm played on. It wasn't the sound that made me act. Not the sound that Captain Alexi had heard on the bridge, nor the one that followed, the one that rent through the air like wrenched metal. It was no mere sound that terrified me, that broke my mind in half. No, it was seven words. The same seven words that I had heard hours before, the ones that had led us to that accursed place. The same seven words that will go with me to my grave.

"God help us all... They are coming!"

The Piper in Yellow

A very long time ago, before the rise of the kings of Aon and the empire of Yorn, a traveler from a distant land came to the country of Edunia. Amongst the broken stone and rotting timbers of that once great kingdom, he stumbled upon a hermit who lived in a hovel of thatch and oak.

"Come," the hermit said to the stranger. "Sit by the fire and warm thyself, for the night is long and it is not often that I receive visitors."

The traveler did as he was bade. The old man brought food and water, and round the fire they sat as the sun sank and the moon rose and a shadow covered the countryside.

"I was lucky to come upon you," said the traveler, "for yours is the only dwelling I have seen for some while, since I entered the vale. There was a village a ways back, a town in the old time. The homes and farms had rotted away, and all that remained of the town-proper were heaps of shattered rock and an ancient church on an overgrown town square."

In the dancing firelight, the old man's eyes shone.

"That would be old Bethlehem," he said. "The people of that town were devout, and the village prosperous. Before *he* came."

"He?"

The hermit rose and walked to a cupboard, removed two tankards, and filled them from a cask on the table.

"All storytelling is a thirsty business," he said as he handed one to the stranger. "But some telling is more thirsty than others.

Come," he said, "sit by the fire. And let us talk of things about which no man should speak…"

* * *

These lands are steeped in time and in mystery. It hangs over them like a heavy shroud, like a fog that never lifts. The domed hills and shadowed vales feel older than they should.

Life flees from here, and most men avoid it. It is not a mindful decision they make, no cold calculus is involved. It is much deeper. It comes from something forgotten. From *somewhere* forgotten.

But whatever the cause, they avoid old Bethlehem. The travelers and merchants do not know why they no longer turn down the road through the glen. Why instead they take the long way round through Fingoyle. They do not choose. They simply do, and their memories escape them. That you would dare to do what they cannot is an enigma unto itself, and what it says of you, only you may know.

But it was not always so.

There was a time when the valley was prosperous, when the game was good and plentiful, the sun shone bright and the crops came up tall and straight. The goods flowed freely down the Brachen Road. The merchants travelled from far kingdoms and all prospered.

It was Beth'lem that prospered most. It had many names you see. Beth'lem. Little Bethlehem. New Bethlehem. Lil'ham. But whatever it was called, its future—straddling the trade road through the vale—seemed assured. So when the plague came, it struck like a judgment from a vengeful God.

It started with the Goodspeed child, a family that lived just beyond the borders of the town. She returned from the forest one night with a cough. Nothing all that unusual for the young. But by the next morning her face had become pallid, and her limbs shook from the cold even as her body burned from fever.

But it was what she saw in her pain-racked nights and febrile waking dreams that sent a chill of fear through the families of the village and drove her poor father mad. She spoke of mountains that walked, of darkness that crawled, and creatures that surround us all, floating unseen and sleeping just beyond the vision of man.

But it was when she spoke of *him* that they feared the most.

"He is coming," she said, that last night before mercy extinguished her flame. The poor child's body went rigid, her eyes focused on some world far beyond our ken. "The watcher at the threshold, the rider on the plain. The sword and the flame. The pestilence and the plague. None will be spared, not from the yellow man." Her eyes fell on her father. "And you, Daddy. You will go first. You will prepare the way."

I cannot say what it was that the accursed father Goodspeed saw in the languid gaze of his only child, but it is said that as he stared into the depths of her soul, his body began to quake, and in one moment of sanity-breaking fear, he leapt to his feet with a shriek and ran from the room. They found his body hanged from a tree by the brook, dead by his own hand, horror still etched upon his face.

That is how it began, with the death of the father, the daughter close on his heels. It did not end there.

Kate Bridges was next, and then Patrick Longlin, and then Stuart Mars. Each one lived just a little closer to Beth'lem than the one before. The pestilence was on the march, and like the great plague that consumed Egypt of old, it cared not for the grown and the aged. The children were its victims, though it made no accounting for first-born, and no blood of the lamb could stave off its fury. When it reached the town-proper, it spread like a field set to the flame.

When the first town child fell ill, the people prayed. By the time they all had—every son or daughter of Beth'lem below the age of 14—the people cried out for anyone, be he god or devil, to save them.

And something heard them, be he god or devil.

He came from the east, the yellow man. Whether because of the robe he wore or his sallow skin, that's what they called him. He was tall of stature, four and a half cubits if he was a span.

He arrived by the Brachen Road. No beast bore him, and had any of the townspeople noticed the flocks of birds winging south at mid-summer, they might have wondered what drove them to take flight.

No watchman met him at the town gate, and he entered without question or hassle. He walked through empty, silent streets, heavy with the stench of pestilence, and a rare smile curved the edges of the stranger's lips. He followed the High Street to the town square and the church that even now holds sway over it. It was there that the townspeople had gathered, beseeching their god to save them from the plague that threatened to take their children.

It was not god that answered them.

Father Johansen was in the middle of prayer—one of many that had gone up that day, buoyed by fear and desperation—when it happened, when the stranger arrived.

"Please, sir," said Father Johansen, always a nervous man but in that moment particularly undone, "this is a house of God."

"God? Does your god answer you now? How long have you prayed?" asked the stranger. "And still your children suffer."

At these words, a murmur swept through the assembly. Who was this man? How could he know that? Might he have the answer to save them?

"That is blasphemy, sir," said the preacher, but there was no conviction in his voice, and by inches he had moved away from the podium.

"I think not. Blasphemy is to speak lies. I speak the truth." The stranger took a step down the aisle, and then another. The feeling in the congregation was as that of a man, standing on a hillside before a storm, the electricity pulsating around him. "I have come from far away, beyond the lake of Hali and the jeweled cities of Carcosa. I have come here, to you, in your time of need." He raised his arm and extended one finger of a boney, blackened hand that stretched forth beyond the sleeve of his cloak. "You worship a broken god, a god that failed. He does not hear your cries. He does not answer them."

There were those in the church that day who, in brasher moments past, filled with drink and with vigor, would have sworn that no man would so curse our Lord without soon meeting Him.

And yet even they sat in silence as the stranger spoke, their fear overawing their religious devotion.

"You cower here. You cry out for salvation. Salvation has arrived. You pray for a deliverer. He stands before you. You ask for a sign. He who has eyes, let him see."

The stranger raised his hand. A shadow fell upon the tabernacle of the Lord. Day became night, and the stream of light from the great stained glass windows ceased. The air grew cold and dense, and tendrils of mist wrapped around the legs of the assembled villagers like cats' tails, and every man and woman it touched felt a little bit of life fade away. There was a deep groan, like the shrieking of wood on a ship in the midst of a storm. Then the shadow lifted as quickly as it had fallen, and the light returned.

"This and much more I will show you, if you so choose."

"Can you save our children?" came a cry from the front. "Can you save my baby?"

"Perhaps. If you are willing to pay."

"So it's money you want," cried another, one who still doubted.

For the first time in their midst, the stranger smiled.

"Oh no, not gold. Not silver. Not jewels or trinkets. Something much more precious. But sacrifice? Yes, sacrifice will be required. A price must be paid. The price of power. And the power you seek is great indeed. So too is the cost."

The stranger sighed, deep and long.

"Now I tire of this place." He turned and almost staggered to the entrance, and it seemed to those who still could bear to look upon him—for many could not, nor could they say why not—that the figure no longer seemed so large, so stately. In fact, he seemed to diminish.

He cast one last glance back at them and said, "Choose, but choose now. I will await your answer at sundown beneath the dead oak that keeps watch over the river bend. Send three men. No more, no less. Sundown."

The doors to the church swung open at his touch, and slammed shut behind him as if carried by a strong wind. The people of the town were left to shiver in the pews, astonished at what they had seen and fearful at what would surely come after.

* * *

As the sun descended, three men were chosen. The Lord Mayor, the Sheriff, and one man who bore no title but was trusted by all, a woodsman who lived in the forests beyond the town proper. All of them had children. All of them had something to lose.

They found the stranger at the bend of the river, on the spot where he had said he would meet them, beneath the branches of the ancient oak. Whatever stature he had lost upon departing the church had returned to him now, and in the growing shadows of a waning day, he was even more fearsome than they remembered.

"And so you came. Are you prepared to pay?"

"Whatever the price," said the Lord Mayor. "For while we are by no means rich, we have enough. And what we have is yours."

"Ah, you listen, but you do not hear. A price must be paid, but it cannot be paid in gold and silver."

The Sheriff stepped forward. "Then what then? My Jeannie is dying and we have not the time for trifles or false hopes."

The stranger grinned, though it felt more like a sneer. "Then to the point, shall we? All for one. The many for the few. All life, for one life."

The Lord Mayor looked to the Sheriff and saw only confusion. It was only the man of the forest who understood.

"Oh my God," the woodsman murmured. "He means to have a sacrifice."

The Sheriff drew his sword. "You are as filled with lies as you are evil."

"Put down your weapon," the stranger said, and as he did he waved his hand before him. To the Sheriff, the weight of the sword became as if he were holding a cart-full of stone. It dropped from his hand, the point driving deep into the ground.

"I have not lied to you. I told you the price was steep, but one well worth paying."

"You want us to kill a child?" The Lord Mayor whimpered. "But why?"

"The plague will not pass on its own. It will lay in the grave all that it touches. To stop it will require a great power. And as power comes only through sacrifice, great power comes only through the greatest of loss."

"We won't do it," said the woodcutter. "I don't believe you can heal them, whatever imposture and parlor tricks you may possess." He gestured at the sword of the Sheriff, still driven into the ground, the other man having no desire to touch it again. "And besides, no one would pay that price."

The stranger stepped forward and stretched out his hand to touch the shoulder of the woodsman. The other man did not flinch. He would show that he was not afraid. But when the stranger touched his arm, he did know fear. The touch was not cold, precisely. Instead, the woodsmen felt empty, as if he had been gutted, everything inside of him ripped away.

"You have a son, do you not? A boy named James? From this moment he is healed. When you go home and see that what I say is true, let that be the answer to your doubt. But it is only temporary. The illness will return to him, unless you do as I say."

"I can't," and the tears began to flow down the granite face of that man, "even for James. I can't trade his life for the life of another."

The stranger lifted his hand from the woodsman's shoulder to touch his cheek, almost caressing him with his cold, bone-thin finger. "Simple creature. You pay that price every day. How many in your trade lay down their lives to build the houses and shops that make up your town? How many have been hanged from this very tree to keep others safe? How many soldiers die at your king's command, for his glory or his treasure or his land?"

"But how can we choose?" said the Lord Mayor. "How can we even begin to pick one of our own?"

The stranger never looked at him, keeping his eyes instead upon the woodsman. "You are a devout man."

"We are all devout men, my lord," interrupted the Lord Mayor. The stranger ignored him.

"Do you remember the story of Jonah and the great fish?"

"Of course," answered the woodsman.

"And when the storm beset the ship in which he hid from your god, how did his companions determine who was to blame?"

"They cast lots."

"Yes, and when the lots fell upon Jonah, they threw him into the sea?"

"They did."

"And did the storm abate?"

"It did."

"Then that is your answer." The sun had fallen, the moon taking its place. Even the wind had died away, and but for their voices, silence held sway. "Go home," said the stranger, "check on your son. See that I speak the truth. Then make your choice."

* * *

The woodsman returned to his home to find his wife in tears. Their only son had been made whole; it could only be called miraculous. The boy's fever had broken just after sunset.

* * *

They gathered in the old church to cast the lots. I can see that you are surprised that they would so decide. Ah, my friend, fear and wonder are powerful drugs, and the townspeople had both in abundance. Fear that their children would die. Wonder that the son of the woodsman had been cured. There was only one who objected, only one who spoke reason in the face of madness.

The woodsman went to the church that evening to plead with his friends and neighbors not to choose a path that could not be unwalked. But the stranger had done more than cure the woodsman's son; he'd robbed him of the faith the people once had in him.

"You have already received the stranger's blessing," said one. "Your child lives, while ours stand on death's doorstep. Why would you deny us what you enjoy?"

The woodsman's pleas for them to hear reason were rebuffed, and soon words turned to shouts, arguments to threats.

The Sheriff stepped forward, his hand on the hilt of his sword. "You've said your piece, woodsman. Now get out."

"He stays," said a voice from the back, and that cold command chilled the blood of all present. The stranger stepped from the daylight beyond into the church. "For the pact must bind you all."

"I won't be a part of it," said the woodsman. "I won't be bound to this."

The stranger chuckled and to all who heard, it sounded like a growl.

"Do you think you have a choice? What in this life led you to that conclusion? You are no island. You are bound to the decisions of the whole. You wish to disagree? The blood of untold women and children slaughtered for the crimes of their cities or their kings mocks your innocence. Stay, or go. It makes no matter. You will be bound."

The woodsman fell silent, and the stranger turned to the congregation.

"Have you made your choice?"

"We have," answered the Lord Mayor.

"And what have you decided?"

"We will do as you ask. Cure our children, and the life of one will be in your hands."

The stranger held his arms high above his head. "So it has been spoken, so you are now bound." Down his hands swung, meeting in one great crash.

Every man and woman in the assembly fell backward as if buffeted by a mighty wind. Many cried out in pain. The woodsman clutched his hand, the agony as if he had grabbed a glowing brand. When he looked down at his palm, he knew why. His skin sizzled, and already, the red, seared flesh had begun to rise—and it formed an image. A ring, with a single point at the bottom of the circle. At its center, three spheres melded together, as if one globe but with three lobes. It was a sigil, one that the woodcutter doubted many had ever seen before. He knew not what it meant, only that it was of a dark and deadly purpose, and that all who gathered that day bore it. The smell of burning flesh hung heavy in the air.

"A spoken oath, sealed in flesh and fire. One you dare not break."

The stranger reached inside his cloak and removed a leather satchel. He threw it at the feet of the Lord Mayor.

"Now your god decides. Inside are circles of marble, one for every family in this town. All are white, save one. He who draws the black sphere, from him shall the sacrifice come."

The stranger turned and made his way to the door of the church. "Where are you going?" cried the Lord Mayor.

"The rest is for you to do," he said without turning. "I go to prepare myself. Tonight I cure your children. Tomorrow I collect my price."

Into the dying light the stranger disappeared.

The lots were cast. It was the son of the Lord Mayor that was chosen.

* * *

That night, the people of Old'ham huddled behind closed doors, clutching their sick children close, praying that the oath they had taken would yield fruit.

It began sometime after midnight. A single sound shattered the perfect stillness of that evening. Some said they heard a child's cry. Others, the shriek of a bird. Still more, the moan of the dying. And others, the wail of an injured beast.

But whatever they heard at first, all agreed about what followed—the sound of piping.

Discordant, yet melodic. Soothing, yet daemonic. A single flute, the music of which did not bring joy. Rather, it seemed to bore into the minds of those who heard it, to steal their happiness and replace it with pain, taking some of their very sanity with it.

And yet as the sound passed, so too did the suffering. In its place came joy, for as the pipe played, the children were healed, one by one. By the time the last note died away, the town had been restored.

The people poured into the streets. They sang, and they danced, and they drank wine. Many things were done beneath the moon that I will not speak of here. But the sun rose, as it must on every night. And when it did, it rose on a day of reckoning.

The stranger came forth. He walked down streets that still echoed with the revelry of the night before. He met no one on his way to the church to collect his prize. He strode up the steps and pushed open the doors.

It was deserted, or at least, that's how it appeared. In an instant, a half-dozen men surrounded him, their swords drawn. The Lord Mayor stepped from behind a pillar, his countenance that of a man who has played another for a fool. But to the Lord Mayor's annoyance, the fool still did not seem to comprehend that he had been played.

"Did you bring the boy?" the stranger asked.

The men chuckled, secure behind the points of their blades.

"Why no, my friend," said the Lord Mayor. "No, I think a new deal is in order. You get to keep your life, and all debts are paid."

"So you mean to break the bargain, then?"

The Lord Mayor took a step forward, drawing his own sword. "Did you not hear me? Your payment is your life. Oh, you had the others fooled, with your trickery and your black magic. But we know how to deal with witches in this town, especially the ones that poison the well and then claim to have the cure. You turn and you go, and if we ever hear of the like of you in these parts again, I will personally ride out and have your head."

The stranger took a step back and into the morning sun. "By your own word, then."

There was a flash of light and smoke, and when the swordsmen opened their eyes again, the stranger was gone.

What came that night became the stuff of legend.

Darkness fell hard and fast, and there were few who thought that it did not come several hours before its appointed time. The moon, a full half the evening before, never rose that night. Ebon night held sway, and silence joined it, the kind that breaks men's minds. But what followed made those who heard it wish that the maddening silence had never been shattered.

It was the sound of piping. But not one pipe. Nay, it was thousands. Drums had joined it. Deep, throbbing drums that pounded into the mind and chased away all thought. A dry wind began to blow, to whip through the streets and rap upon the doors. A chorus of screams was added to the cacophony. Those howls of pain were no illusion, however; they were very much of this earth.

Hell had come to Old'ham, the Devil seeking his due.

In his home in the forests, the woodsman heard all. His family huddled in fear, but he took up his sword. They begged him not to go, but when the woodsman looked to the mark upon his hand, he knew that he had a duty to stop whatever the townspeople had so foolishly started. He rushed into the darkness to the fate that awaited him.

By the time he reached the church, the roar of satanic song and the pitiful cries of the dying and those who wished they were dead had become an almost solid wall of sound. But when he turned the corner and ran into the High Street, it was then that his sanity almost slipped.

A great beast filled the city street. Or at least, that is how he perceived it. One moment, it was a monster, unlike anything he had ever seen before, with whip-like arms that buzzed and slapped against the earth in great thunderous strikes. Then it was a column of smoke and fire that roared and burned and spat out noxious fumes. Then it was a dragon, a great black dragon with the arms and wings of a bat. Then it was a swirling vortex of wind and dust that ripped apart all in its path. But whatever form it took, the piping never ceased, nor did the beating of the drums.

As he watched, the form, whatever form it was at the moment, continued its slow march toward him. A door would swing open or a wall would be torn down, the inhabitants therein vomited out into the streets screaming and gibbering and clawing at the ground. Before him they were sliced in half by a crashing, caber-like arm; snapped up by the jaws of an enormous maw, ripped apart by a whirlwind, or turned to ash by toxic vapors. The end was always the same; they all died. All of them—men, women, and children.

The woodsman dropped his sword. He stepped forward. "You want a sacrifice!" he screamed. "Take me."

The swirling chaos before him halted. Then it seemed to part, and out stepped the stranger. His amber cloak billowed like smoke, and in his hand he held a small flute.

"Woodsman, you would offer yourself as a sacrifice?"

The woodsman hesitated but for a moment. He closed his eyes and uttered a prayer to God—both the one that he worshiped, and those to whom his ancestors bowed before beyond the veil.

"Yes," he said. "I am ready."

There was a rumble that shook the earth. It came from the stranger. He was laughing. "Do you not see?" he said, sweeping his arm behind him as if to encompass the entire town. "Do you still not understand? What is the sacrifice of one, when I can have hundreds? You offer yourself now. But these, they offered themselves before. They swore the oath that you rejected. A blood bond, to make full the debt they owed if it were not paid—with interest accrued."

"But I am bound as well," the woodsman said, almost begging. "Take me instead."

"What does your life mean to me? I have lived a thousand of your lifetimes. Do you think I care for you, or this accursed place? Their blood gives me power, and one day, when it runs like rivers, when the power is enough, then I will use it to change the very course of the stars in the sky. And when they are right, all will bow before their true masters."

The woodsman looked down to the sword that still lay in the dust. The stranger began to laugh again.

"You are a fool. But I must say, bravery such as this I have rarely seen from your kind. Go back to your family. Tell them you love them. And then send them away, your wife and your child. This I give to you, but you must give me something in return. I will come for you. When I finish here."

Then he turned and stepped back into the storm.

The woodsman ran home. He hugged his wife and child tight, and then he told them to run, to flee to the next town and then the one beyond that and not to stop until they reached a place where no one had ever heard of Old Bethlehem. They did not protest. They knew that death was on their doorstep. They knew that this was their only chance. I hope that wherever they fled, they lived out their lives in peace and joy.

The stranger came to the house of the woodsman. The roof did not fly away. The wall did not collapse. Instead, there was merely a knock on the door.

The woodsman opened it.

The stranger stood before him.

"To you," he said, "I grant my pardon, be it on one condition. Here you will stay, and you will spread to all those who pass by my story. You will tell them what came to be in this town, so that all may fear the name of Nyarlathotep, the Piper in Yellow!"

* * *

You see, my friend, I am the man who spoke with death that day, all those centuries ago. And this mark upon my hand is the sigil of my mission—and my curse.

You seem confused? Oh, you've never heard of the story of the piper? Well, I suppose the details change in the retelling, and there are many who stray within these borders and then go on to their homes or to far horizons who no doubt soften the edges, for the sake perhaps of their own sanity.

And of course, there's the name of the town itself. For I told you that, whatever its fathers may have wished, Bethlehem never really stuck. So it bears many names, in tales and in song. But there is one that is most prominent. One that seems to fit Lil'ham more than most. A strange thing really, for it is not only a corruption but an inversion.

Most people have never heard of Bethlehem or New Bedlam or Lil'ham.

No, in the story that gets retold the most, the story that most people have heard, the town went by another name—

Hamelin.

The Worm That Conquers

Letters from Lieutenant François le Villard to Mademoiselle Marguerite Deraismes (Translated), February 18 – March 21, 1916

My dearest Marguerite,

How I wish that I could see you again, if even for a moment. I know you are with me always, and when I close my eyes, it is your face I see. Sometimes I think that I catch a glimpse of you, walking amongst the fog and iridescent mist beyond the trenches, as if your spirit has traveled from Étretat to be with me as you sleep safely in your bed. But then the cannon fires and the earth quakes and my reverie is chased away.

The battlefield is no place for a dreamer.

There are those who would tell me that I should not so freely share with you the things that I have seen, the things that I have feared, the deaths I have almost died and may yet face. With the deepest respect, they are fools.

I know you worry for me. I know that it eats you away inside. Is it better to lie to you, to deny to you the truth? You have seen the death notices in the papers. You are no fool. And that is why I love you. So until that day comes when you tell me you wish not to hear of the things I see, I shall deliver them to you.

As clearly and truthfully as I can.

* * *

When I dream, I do not dream of war. I do not hear the cannonade. I do not see the arcs of fire. I do not feel their heat. Their crash does not shake me. I do not know where I go, precisely. Only that I am away. That I am absent. Without leave. Where there is no muck and mire. Where blood and stagnant water do not mix and mingle. Where the mud does not flow like a narrow sea, where death does not guard the shore.

That is my dream. Life is my nightmare.

* * *

There are rumors circulating among the men. I hear them, even though they speak only in hushed tones which drop to silence when I am nearby. There are times I wish I was an enlisted man. Soldiers may follow a lieutenant into fire and death, but they will never truly trust him. Still, I hear what I am not meant to.

They say that the Germans know they cannot win, that these endless lines of torn earth will never break. One might mistake this lack of confidence as a positive development, but such rumors seldom are. The men whisper of a new plan, to bleed us white. To deal death in such numbers that our will to fight is broken, even if our lines still hold. And they say that is why we have been sent here, to this place called Verdun.

To be bled.

* * *

The rain came down in torrents. The fog that rose up from the bog that lies between the lines was so thick that if the Germans had marched a division across the mud-sea we would not have known it until they were driving bayonets into our chests. But nothing moves out there. Nothing marches in the howling wind. Still, we wait and we stand guard. The rain pouring, soaking uniforms and men's souls. The water pools at our feet, eating away at them. Rotting them from the inside, while the rats are forced from their holes, scurrying along the edge of the parapets, grown fat and slow from the flesh of the dead.

My eyes have become accustomed to the darkness. To move in daylight is to invite death, and we have become creatures of the night. The pacifists and the philosophers say that war turns men into animals. They are wrong. War makes monsters of us all.

* * *

The Germans hold the high ground. Our aerial reconnaissance reports that they have placed artillery upon those heights. From there they will rain down fire upon us. And we will try to take those hills to stop them. Against that insignificant mound, the flower of France shall dash itself until we wash it away in our blood.

* * *

They came for us at midnight, rising up out of the mist, fire like dragons' eyes. We had been expecting them, and yet we were not ready for our expectations to turn to that horror.

Every evening we had waited, eyes peering into the shrouded night, wondering much, seeing little. I had command of a three-man Hotchkiss crew, and all of us peered over the barrels of our machine guns, certain that what the mud slowed and the barbed wire stopped, we could kill.

That was the plan from command, at least. Let the Germans come. Let them weaken themselves. And then we would counter, break their lines, take the hill.

I wonder how many such flights of military fancy were formed in the bowels of command bunkers along the front. How often generals and colonels pushed imaginary units across imaginary lines to imaginary goals with a sureness that the real men they represented would somehow turn that fancy into fact. Would turn chalk symbols on a blackboard into gains on the ground. Would turn a pin pushed into a map into the end of the war.

The Germans had maps, too. And they were just as careless.

So we waited. Some might think that the waiting would dull the senses, that day after day and night after night of anticipation would lead to complacency. Not so, not there, not in the trenches.

Every night our nerves bristled, electric with the coming fight. We stared out over that endless dead plain and longed for daylight.

Tonight, though, should have been safe. The rains had fallen all day, and we doubted, in our hearts if not in spoken words, that the enemy would come. The fog was thick upon the field of battle. Nothing moved there in the swirling mists, at least, nothing we saw.

But they were there. Creeping along. Crawling, when they should have walked. Beneath the death-shroud gray fog.

They rose as one.

At first, we did not see them. We had stared so long into the darkness that our eyes were masked, as if covered in scales. Then we saw the light, and the scales fell away.

I'll never know, of course, what the others saw in that moment. No doubt that vision was for each man's eyes alone. All I know is this—in an instant, No Man's Land erupted in fire.

There were several hundred of them, perhaps a thousand feet from the parapet, spread down the line as far as the eye could see in either direction. They stood like Prometheus, each with one arm above his head, fire in his hand. Or that is how I saw them, at least, as gods come to earth, to illuminate the night and cleanse the battlefield of the muck and the filth with which we had covered it.

Every man in the trenches stood dumbstruck by what we witnessed. But it was no angel, no god, no deliverer. It was death.

"You fools!" I shouted, as much at my own stupidity as at my men. "Kill them!"

But it was too late. From the hills above, German artillerymen had zeroed in their guns. The flares the soldiers held above their heads gave them the ultimate marker. I didn't even get off a shot before the first shell fell. Instead, I grabbed my machine gunner and threw him to the ground.

The first shell exploded a hundred yards down the trench. Close enough that I saw men torn to pieces, close enough that I could hear the screams of the dying. But not so close as to put us in danger. That would come later. The first shell was the last one I really saw. There were too many that followed too quickly.

They crashed down like bolts from the thunder god, ripping apart our lines, bursting eardrums, shattering bone, shredding skin. A man cannot think in a moment of horror like that, and in my mind's eye I saw a kaleidoscope of images, flashes of my past, both familiar and unfamiliar days. A field behind my family's home on a summer eve. A girl at the Exposition Universelle, a flower in her hair. The sun half-obscured by clouds. A wooden stick, swirling in a whirlpool. Around and around and around. But never down. You, on the night of our wedding, your skin glistening in the moonlight, the half-smile on your face.

Thunder was our world, and in the maelstrom men screamed. Some called to their God, to their mothers, while others shouted words in tongues primeval, left-over languages long forgotten.

How long did the shells fall? Was it minutes? Hours? Perhaps days, for if the sun had risen and fallen in that mind-shattering span I would not have known it, nor felt its warmth upon my face. You will never know, thank God, what it feels like to believe that every second could be your last and to expect that the next one will be.

But I did not die, and like a storm that rolls across the plain and into someone else's future, the thunder ceased. Of the men who lived, some cowered in the trenches, unwilling to believe that it had really ended. Others pulled themselves up, their eyes void of all understanding. But most started to celebrate. They had survived, and their cries of joy might have reached all the way to Heaven.

Fools.

I grabbed my gunner up from the pit in which he lay. He shook in my hands, and I am ashamed to say that I struck him across the mouth to calm him. I could think of no other way, and that act of violence brought him back. "Man your weapon," I said. Then I blew the whistle hanging from my neck. Even in their reveries, to that unmistakable signal they responded. Many turned to me, so conditioned were they to answer to that sound.

"Prepare for the attack!"

I saw it in their eyes, the recognition—the bombardment was only the beginning.

The racket of rifles clacking along the parapet filled the air. From the rear came reinforcements, men pressed into action as the generals realized what was coming. With them, the stretcher carriers, Charons of the battlefield, the bravest men I have ever known.

The trenches had become smoking pits. For as far as I could see the left line was shattered, and men were working to rebuild the walls in the precious few moments we had. The right was secure; the guns had overshot. It was a blessing, but I knew those further back in camp had suffered for our good fortune.

We gazed into the smoke and haze and darkness. The only sounds were of picks and shovels, of shouts of men to dig faster. In the end there would be no time. The roar of shouting erupted before their guns did.

Then it was chaos and sound and shooting and blood and death and fire and madness. A man in battle is no longer a man. He does not think as a man thinks. He does not fear as a man fears. He becomes a machine, an animal that acts on instinct and training, that kills without regret, that dies without knowledge or consideration.

The storm-driven sea of Germans crashed upon the rocks of our lines. My gunner fired without ceasing, as I fed him belt after belt of ammo and poured the contents of several canteens upon the barrel that glowed red-hot. I threw back grenades without thinking. I killed men at point-blank range. I faced death more times than I can recall or could ever have imagined. Hours became as minutes, and it was only when the sun broke above the plain of dead and dying that I knew how much time had passed. The attack was over.

* * *

I have heard the most remarkable story, and I must share it with you, even as I now question the wisdom of our agreed-upon candor.

As is custom, those of us who survived the attack were rotated off the front line for a few days of relative relaxation in the city of Verdun, if one can rest with the sound of the guns always in one's ears. It is perhaps unsurprising that the only place where one might find a reprieve from the battlefield is the local tavern.

One night, when a storm hid the noise of cannon fire with heavenly thunder, I stumbled upon the story which I now relate. I had entered the tavern, intent upon nothing more than a glass of wine before I retired. It was a rustic place, the ceiling blackened by decades of pipe smoke and oil lamps that still hung from rafters. They swung gently, as if softly touched by the tremors from the fall of each shell miles away. Shadows danced upon the walls, and I followed them to a gathering of men, all of whom I knew well.

They were surrounding a sergeant, Nicholas Couchet, a man whom I had come to know as not only a fine soldier but as a loyal friend. And yet there was a feverish look about him that I did not recognize and did not like. The fire in his eyes burned with a quiet intensity, the lines of his mouth quivered, and I knew that whatever he spoke of now to these men was not something he would have so freely shared with me.

As I approached, he fell silent, and the men about him began to scatter.

"No, stay," I said gently, "I didn't mean to interrupt." Something of my words or my demeanor must have calmed them, for I saw the tension relax in their shoulders as they allowed themselves to fall back into their seats. Only Nicholas still appeared nervous.

"Lieutenant," he said, "to what do we owe the honor of your presence?"

I pulled out a chair and slid into it. My glass of wine was full, but their tankards of ale were empty. I turned to the bar and ordered another round for them all.

"That's very kind of you, sir, but the night has grown old, and I best be making my way."

"No, no, Nicholas, please. Stay at least until you finish your drink. Besides, I noticed that you were regaling the men with some tale, and I thought I might hear it myself."

He glanced to either side of him, but if it was in supplication to his fellows, none of them stepped forward to save him.

"It's nothing that would interest you, sir," he said. "Just gossip amongst the enlisted men."

"And since when have you and I stood on rank? Let's have it. I could use a distraction."

He drew in a breath and sighed long and deep. That fire came back into his eyes, but this time I recognized it as fear.

"I've always respected you, Lieutenant Villard, and I suppose I've taken the notion that you respect me too, as much as a gentleman such as yourself might have such feelings toward a man like me. And I hope, after I tell you what you want to hear, that you'll still respect me."

I nodded, now both unsure of what was about to be revealed to me and somewhat unsettled by the possibilities.

"There are rumors spreading amongst the men," he said, almost in a whisper. "Stories, mad ones I would say, did I not know the sort who have related them, had I not seen some of the evidence with my own eyes."

He must have detected a look of concern flash across my face, for he paused then, and I had to urge him to continue.

"Go on."

"Something walks in No Man's Land," he said. "Something that the bombardment awoke. Something that shouldn't be, but is."

I was, of course, incredulous, but the look on Nicholas's face—his eyes wide, his skin blanched, his eyebrows raised high—cut off any thought that this might be a jest. More serious concerns presented themselves, that perhaps Nicholas had been broken by the bombardment, that a career spanning decades and dressed in the highest honors might have come crashing down around him.

"I know what you must be thinking, sir," he said, "but in my days I have seen enough to believe that there are things beyond our ken. Things that neither you nor I can understand, that they do not teach in universities and that cannot be found in books. At least, none that any Christian would dare to read."

"All right," I said. "Just what have you heard?"

"It started after the first bombardment, the one that you so honorably endured. They say that there has ne'er been one of its like, not in this war or any war to ever scar the face of earth. Something was uncovered, or awoken, or some door opened that was always meant to stay shut. But whatever the cause, strange things have started happening all along the lines."

"What sort of things?"

"It started with a mist," he said, "a fog unlike any that the men had ever seen. It crept across the broken fields when the battle was over, but it glowed green with its own light, even on a night when there was no moon and the stars were shrouded in cloud. They thought at first it was a weapon, some gas the Germans had released. But it came and did no harm to man nor beast. But it shone with that devil's fire, lying thick and putrid on all the land."

Of this one thing, I could not argue, for I had seen the green fog before our unit was relieved. "I assume there was more to it than unusual weather," I said.

"Aye," he said, "much more. Private Étienne, tell the Lieutenant what you saw."

A rosy-cheeked lad who could not have been more than sixteen if he was a day stepped forward, his cap clutched in his hand.

"It's all right, lad," Nicholas said. "Just tell it true."

"The day after the battle," he began, his voice cracking as he spoke, "two German officers came to headquarters under a flag of truce. They wanted to know what we did with the bodies."

"The bodies?"

"Yes, the Germans who had been killed in the fighting."

"I don't understand."

"They were missing, you see. When the German stretcher bearers went into the field, they only found a handful of men, far fewer than there should have been. Far fewer than they had expected, given their losses. And some of the ones they did find were, well..."

He looked down at his hands, and I noticed for the first time that they were shaking. Nicholas slid a tankard of ale over toward him. He took it and gulped it, almost greedily.

"They were mutilated," he said finally. "And not like you would expect. Not from bullets or even bombs. From something else they couldn't explain. The Germans were very angry. They said that we had violated every law of war and human decency.

The commander denied it all, of course. He threw them out, and told them that the next time he saw them he'd have them arrested."

"Which is understandable," Nicholas said. "Who would believe such a thing? But three nights ago we launched an offensive against the heights, to take the German guns. The results were..." Nicholas glanced at the men, mostly boys, who surrounded him and remembered his place, "a good beginning. But our losses were also steep."

The young man piped up again. "The stretcher bearers went out as soon as the ceasefire was called. Most of them were very busy. All but the ones in Quadrant C. In C, there was no one."

"No one?" I said.

"The commander thought it was the Germans, retaliating for what they said we had done with their dead and wounded. He said that they had done it on purpose to spite us. But I'm not so sure."

"Why not? Would you put anything beyond them?"

"No," he said, "of course not. But there was no time. Not to carry that many men away. Whatever took them did so quickly and quietly. Like a spirit."

"Or a demon," someone chimed in from the back.

"Or a monster," said another.

"Oh, come now," I said. I was unnerved, but I have seen many things in this war to unnerve me, and I have come to understand that the only real job of an officer is to never show his fear to his men. "This is a German ploy. They know they cannot break us with arms, so they will break our spirit instead with tricks and stories of ghosts in the darkness."

"Perhaps," said Nicholas, and I could tell that I alone truly believed it. "But watch yourself out there, Lieutenant. There's more to fear in No Man's Land than German bullets."

* * *

I must be brief. Our unit has been ordered back to the front lines to prepare for an attack on the heights. I don't have to tell you, my darling, what that means. I love you. I love you with all my heart, all my soul. And if this is to be my end, then I will die with your name on my lips.

*   *   *

I have seen the darkness that haunts men's dreams, and I pray for the dawn. But even when—if?—it comes, the sun itself cannot chase away the shadow that falls over me.

I am writing from a shell crater deep within the dead zone, halfway between our lines and the Germans'. A boy named Joseph once lay beside me, shot through the throat. He is dead now, but it wasn't the bullet that killed him.

The army arrayed at dusk, miles of men and guns, bayonets gleaming in the dying light of the last day for so many. Row upon row of helmets, like corn in a field, stretching forever, awaiting the thresher.

The attack began at twilight.

We poured across the broken field, the mad shouts and hurrahs of boys fresh from the cities cut short by the *rack-y-tac-tac* of German machine guns. Sappers cut barbed-wire and blew hardened positions. Artillery shells filled the sky and crashed down ahead of us. Rangers hit machine-gun nests, and raiders dropped into forward trenches and slashed and stabbed and lobbed grenades.

Forward we pressed, as bullets passed and men died and the ground grew sodden with the tramp of a thousand feet and the gentle rain of blood. We reached the German heights. We went no farther. All of man's greatness, all of his genius, all that he has harnessed and achieved, distilled into the fragmentation grenade and the 8mm cartridge and the Big Bertha heavy-artillery gun.

Our lines faltered, then stopped, then broke. The bugles sounded. The retreat began. We fell away, a receding wave. Back, back, back.

Halfway home, between Heaven and Hell, I caught a round in the shoulder that spun me like a top before it passed through my flesh to bury itself in the dirt. It carried me forward with it, throwing me into the shell crater where I now lay. Joseph, bless his foolishness, turned to me. He started to say something, to check on me, I suppose. But a German somewhere pulled the trigger on his gun a split second earlier, and the words were drowned in lead and gore. Joseph's throat exploded. The artery within pulsed and a stream of blood arched through the darkness and splashed into my face, stinging my eyes. Joseph collapsed beside me, his hand to his neck.

I was covered in Joseph's blood. I could taste the metallic tang deep in my throat. I staunched his wound as best I could, and we waited, his life slipping away and me trying to hold onto it. I prayed for daylight. The sun would rise, the battle would end, and the stretcher men would come. We had only to survive the night.

The sounds of war faded, save for the occasional crack of a sniper's rifle. Enough to keep us down, even if Joseph weren't bleeding to death in my arms. Eventually, even the sniper fire died away. It was just Joseph's ragged breathing and the sound of my own heart.

Hours passed. I could not help but notice that the same strange, green fog I had witnessed days earlier had grown thick and unyielding on the battlefield. I had little time to consider it, though. With every passing moment, I worried that help might not make it in time for dear Joseph. And then something happened that made that fear seem like the obsession of a child.

It began with a sound which I am not certain can be described, but I will do as best I can. It was a clicking sound, like claws on a tile floor, or scales sliding across each other. I tried to tell myself it was some kind of weapon, something we had not seen before, but it was a lie. I knew better. And whatever it was, it was coming closer.

I peered over the edge of the shell crater. Something moved in the mist.

I blinked, wishing it away. And yet it was there, and inching toward us. It stayed low and tight to the ground. It slid across the earth like the shadow of a Nieuport flying above at midday. But there was no light to cast that shade. It was a thing, like a man lying upon his belly, slithering, the blackest cloak ever put through the loom trailing behind.

I stared at it, stupidly, unable to take my eyes off of that specter, that ghoul. And then what I perceived to be its head tilted up, and it looked squarely upon me.

I dropped, sliding down the slope of the crater wall, praying to God that it had not seen me. Silence closed in. My heartbeat thrummed with such violence that I was afraid whatever was out there could hear it. When Joseph moaned beside me, I am ashamed to write I drew my pistol, though what I intended to do with it I cannot say. To hush him perhaps? Even if I were so selfish, I would have been equally foolish. In that hell-quiet my gun would have sounded like thunder.

In the end, it didn't matter.

A moment later, it was upon us. It rose above the edge of the crater, a thing like a man in form only. Its hands were claws, skeletal and ragged. I might say that its face was something like a corpse, but even that would not do justice to the horror I beheld — noseless, its mouth a gapping maw, what passed for eyes burning like flames in its skull.

It swept down the ledge, and I did fire my gun then, though the bullet either passed through it or simply did nothing to stop it. It fell upon me, and the stench was such that I could not draw a breath. It crawled along my body, slithering like a snake. It seemed as though it breathed deeply of me, its face millimeters from the wound in my shoulder. Then it drew away sharply, and, fixing me with its gaze again, I would swear, were it not madness made manifest, that it said something.

Joseph, poor Joseph. It noticed him. It spun away from me, sliding across the ground. It breathed deeply again, but this time it did not hesitate. It fell upon the boy. He screamed only once, but even that was quickly stifled. I could not move. I could do nothing to save him. And I could not look away. I watched as this thing seemed to suck him dry, as blood and viscera and God knows what else splattered across the shell crater.

As quickly as it began, it ended. The thing slid over the top of the crater, carrying Joseph with it. Then it was gone.

I sit here, waiting, alone, for dawn to come. I know I made a solemn vow to you that I would hide nothing from your eyes. But in writing this letter, I know that this is too much. I will take this story with me to my grave, and if anyone finds these words here in this field, know from their telling that No Man's Land is not empty, but that it is no man that walks upon it.

* * *

Journal of Henry Armitage, July 26, 1933

Long we sat, listening to the inspector's words, and the sudden hunger that struck me as he finished spoke to the hours that had passed. But in that time, Villard had become one of us.

"They found me the next morning, of course. Delirious, gibbering about things that walked in the mist and devoured the dead and the dying. No one ever believed me, but I know what I saw. I spent a few weeks in a field hospital and then was promoted, for gallantry. I bided the rest of the war at headquarters, away from the front, away from the fighting.

"So I can tell you one thing for certain, gentlemen. I do not know if what you say is madness or prophecy. But I do know this. Evil is real, and it is horrible, and it must be confronted and defeated. So if you go forth on this crusade, then I will march with you, even if it is to our own destruction. It is a march I have made before."

Carter stood and clapped him on the shoulder. "Then we go together to Normandy, and we go now. Once more into the breach, and we will either return with the staff, or we will not return at all. On those shores, the fate of mankind will be decided."

As we stood to leave for the grand station in the heart of Paris, I turned back to the inspector, for I had one last question.

"You said that the creature spoke to you, before it took your friend."

"Yes."

"What did it say?"

The inspector glanced at his hands, and I suppose I was surprised that they were not shaking. Then he looked back at me.

"I can't be sure, of course, for I only heard the barest whisper. But I thought it said three words...

"'Not...yet...ripe.'"

The Wind Passes Like a Fire

When the wind comes to the city, it blows dry...and hot. It creeps up quietly. Sneaking up behind you, like a thief or an old friend. Sometimes it tickles your senses, caresses your neck. Other times it hits hard, like a slap in the face. It brings the smell of heat, the taste of dust. It nuzzles your legs like kittens. It nips at your heels like dogs. It pats you on the back, it rubs you on the stomach. It surrounds you, envelops you, embraces you. Makes you sweat.

That's how it was that summer, like all summers, when it came. Slowly at first. Trickling down the mountains, dancing down Mulholland, sweeping through its dark corners, its hidden places. Loping down Sunset and Cahuenga. Furtively, secretly. But then with a roar, a howl. The wind came, like it always did. But that summer, it was different.

The wind carried more than the dust, more than the heat. It brought a shadow, a cloak of fear, a shroud of secrets. We all heard it. Heard its murmured warnings, its whispered cries. Then we saw it.

On the news, at first. And when we saw the stories our first reaction was laughter and smiles. A joke, it seemed, hallucinations of drug-addled minds. Reports of a wild animal in the hills, they said. The Beast of La Brea some called it, mostly in jest. But then they stopped laughing.

It was the animals that were struck first. Starting with the small ones. The birds, the squirrels. And then the dogs and cats. Disappeared without a trace. Without blood, without remains, without struggle, without sound. No one ever saw who or what did it. No one ever knew where the victims went.

There were rumors, of course. Twice told tales. A girl might mention that her best friend's boyfriend swore he saw a shadow move across his backyard, the night the family dog went missing. Probably a coyote, someone would reply. And that was good enough for a while. But then it wasn't just dogs and cats.

It seemed I overheard a different story every day. In cafes and coffee shops, in beauty parlors and boutiques.

"Did you hear about the Johnsons?" they'd ask.

"What about them?"

"They're gone."

"Gone? Where did they go?"

"Nobody knows. One day they were there, the next they weren't."

"What do you mean?"

"I mean what I said. One day they were there. Becky Johnson went to school. Dave Johnson went to work. Alice Johnson stayed home. The next day, they didn't."

"Did someone call the police?"

"Of course someone called the police."

"What did they say?"

"They don't know. They say that when they got to their house, everything was in order. Nothing was out of place. They even fixed breakfast."

"Breakfast?"

"Yeah. If you believe what you hear, the coffee was still hot."

"That's impossible."

"I just know what I hear."

And so it went. I'd walk down the street, my street, in Silver Lake, like I did every summer. The wind would blow around me, tickle my senses, carry me along like a kite on a string. But every day it seemed the people on the street were just a little bit fewer, just a little bit less. Where they went, I didn't know. Whether they hid in their houses in fear, cowering behind locked doors. Or whether there was no one left to cower.

There was an old man. He used to stand on the corner of Griffith Park and Hyperion and sell fresh fruit. Some days it seemed like he was the only one left.

"Business is slow," he'd say. "Business is slow, and I think it's gonna get slower."

"Why do you say that?" I'd ask. He'd just chuckle.

"You know as well as I. Look around. Where are they going?"

"Away, I guess."

"That much's certain. It's the wind, you know."

"The wind?"

"It came down different this year."

"What do you mean?"

"Just came down different. Like it had a purpose. Like it had a hunger. It'll take us all, I suppose. The wind. Before it's gone."

"But it's just the wind," I pleaded.

"Ain't it always just the wind? Or is that just what we tell ourselves. When we hear or see something we can't explain. But sometimes…sometimes it's more."

The next day, the old man was gone.

But the wind remained. Blowing through the empty roads, the alleys. Swirling in deserted parks. Parading down abandoned subway tunnels. No one to kiss. No one to touch. No one but me.

I don't know why it's left me. Don't know what I'll do now, either. I went to my old school yesterday. There was no one there. No teachers. No students. No parents. Truth is, my mom and dad disappeared a week ago. They didn't leave a note. They didn't even take the car. I guess I didn't want to believe it, not at first. There's no denying it now.

The electricity still works. The plant's running on its own. But how long will that last? How long can it? It'll go soon. And when it does, the world will go dark. But the wind still knows the way.

I turn on the TV every now and then, just to see. There's nothing on, of course. You might have thought there would have been an emergency broadcast at least, but there's not. Whether it happened so slow that no one noticed or whether the world didn't want to see, it all ended with a whimper, not a bang. Just the blank blackness of electricity on a screen.

Truth is, I don't know if there is anyone else left in all the world. I took the car yesterday to the city. Right to the heart of it. I don't know what I thought I would find. But I know what I hoped to see. Death, destruction, blood. Signs of a disaster. A disaster I could understand. A disaster my mind could take. But that's not what I saw. Not at all.

It was quiet, empty, and perfectly in order. It was as if the city went to sleep and never woke up. The same as everywhere else. Perfect silence, perfect stillness. Except for the wind. Running down the streets. Brushing through the palms.

I didn't come back till it was almost dark. As I pulled the car into the drive, I thought I saw a shadow move behind me. I tried to make it out, as much as you can with a shadow. Can't say I saw much, but I guess my mind made up for what I couldn't see. And in my mind, I saw a beast. A great stalking terror. With massive shoulders, loping on all fours. Fiery eyes and sharp teeth.

"It's just the wind," I murmured to myself. Just the wind, blowing through my mind. Casting shadows on my soul.

I don't know what I'll do now. I guess I'll wait. The same fate awaits all men, right? In the end? I guess the same fate awaits me, too. When will it come? I don't know. Why does it wait? I can't say. But I do know this.

When the wind comes to the city, it blows dry…and hot.

The Lost Class of Miskatonic University

Let me set the scene. The year is 1715. Queen Anne's War has concluded only a couple years before. The raiding of two nearby Wampanoag villages by Arkham militia ended native resistance, but not their thirst for revenge or the suspicion the white settlers hold for them. A cloud lays over Arkham: of doubt, of anger, of fear. It is into this dark miasma that twenty students entered when they came to Miskatonic that season, looking forward to a year of academic delights, blissfully unaware of the doom that hung over them. Everything came to a head on All Hallows Eve.

I'll start with what we know, or at least, what history teaches us. The official record comes from a sensational story printed in the Boston News-Letter on November 12. That story paints a graphic picture of a violent storm that had befallen Arkham on the evening of October 31. It was late in the season for such a storm, yet it raged from the falling of the sun till its rising. When the storm cleared on the morning of the first, Arkham men who had gone out to survey the damage stumbled upon an unusual scene at Miskatonic College. The professors were in a state of panic. Having left their homes to check on the twenty students who were in attendance that year, they could find no one. Not on the grounds. Not in their living quarters. None of the students had turned up in the town proper, either.

The Arkham men conducted their own search. They found nothing out of place in any of the students' rooms. No signs of struggle. No evidence of break-ins. It was as if they simply disappeared.

Arkham and College authorities fathomed only one conclusion—the local natives, the Wampanoag, had come under cover of storm and spirited away the students. A raiding party was formed, and Wampanoag villages burned. But no trace was ever found of the boys.

It's strange, then, that Miskatonic has never acknowledged the fate of the class of 1715, never erected a monument to those who perished, never memorialized their names. In fact, you can find no record of the events, save in the tattered pages of the Boston News-Letter archives. Some claim that the truth is far less romantic, that Miskatonic simply failed to open that year, that ecclesiastical disputes, of all things, led to a strike that was not resolved until the fall of 1716. But how then does one explain that strange story that riveted the people of Boston? True, the press was even less reliable in those days, even more likely to engage in supposition, superstition, and sensationalism. But to make up the story out of whole cloth?

And that's the rub, my friends. As Professor Wade has said, there is truth in all legends. I found the truth in a journal, written by one of the Arkham men who came to Miskatonic that dark day, and who found his nights—and his dreams—haunted by what he saw there. The terrible story relayed by the Boston News-Letter? It was wrong all right. It barely scratched the surface of the horror that befell this place.

The man who wrote the journal was Arthur Belknap. He was a blacksmith, a simple but honorable man who had attained a position of leadership and respect in the community. When the strange mystery of October 31 began to envelop the town of Arkham, he knew it would fall on him to unravel it.

Belknap wrote that there was no storm that day. That was the first of the inconsistencies. A chill was in the air instead, and from the waters of the Miskatonic a thick fog had rolled in. Nothing unusual about that, not for that time of the year. And yet, Belknap did not like that fog. He could not say why, couldn't put his finger on it. But he felt it, in his bones, in that deep part of your brain that you best not ignore.

A ship's captain would later relate to him that he had seen the birth of that fog as it arose from Arkham Harbor. He had marked it then as an ill omen, more so when he saw it gather at the mouth of the Miskatonic River, gather and then creep inexorably toward the town. Creeping—against the wind.

The mist spread over Arkham, and the few people who had ventured out that evening fled its coming. Belknap himself took in another man, a tavern keep named Jeremiah Prim, who could not make his own dwelling before the bank of fog overtook him. As he stepped across the threshold, he clasped Belknap on the arms, and in his eyes was a gratitude so deep that Belknap had only seen it one other time in his life, when he pulled a sailor gone overboard from the sea. And yet somehow, even the terror of the deep did not compare to what came stalking down the street just beyond his door.

In his journal Belknap recorded that as it passed over and around them, he felt for the first time in his life as if he were cut off from God, as if he stood alone against some horror he could not fathom and could never hope to defeat. It was not simply that the fog blocked out the full moon that had risen earlier that night, he wrote. Rather, it was as if that moon no longer hung in the sky above them. As if there was no sky at all, beyond the mist. Or perhaps it was that there was *nothing* beyond it, that the thick tendrils of gray smoke that seemed to move with a purpose down the cobblestone street, caressing the windows—or licking them even, Belknap had thought with a shudder—had devoured all the world, and would devour them, too.

Belknap's mind went back to Exodus, to the ten plagues of Egypt and the Passover, when the angel of death, the finger of a vengeful God, cast his shadow upon the people of the Nile. The old blacksmith knew what he saw that day was something very much like that; death was in the cloud, and any who would open his door and invite that visitor in would not live to close it. But Belknap knew something else, too. It was not God that walked in the shadow. Not his God, at least.

"'Tis of the devil," Prim murmured. Belknap did not rebuke him, even if he didn't precisely agree with him either. The groaning of the timbers above chilled him, and his eyes followed Prim's to the ceiling. A scrabbling, a scratching, trickled down to them, as of a thousand clawed hands scrambling across the roof. The timbers creaked again, and dust shook down into Belknap's eyes.

It'll never hold, he thought, *and then whatever walks—or crawls—above, whatever lives in the cloud, will come to take us.* But the beams that Belknap had laid with his own hands did hold, and so did the roof. Just as the night became darkest, a single ray of light cut the mist, shining through Belknap's window. As quickly as the mist had come, it passed on, and Belknap felt the heaviness, the weight of something immeasurable, lift from him. He walked to the door, grabbed the handle.

"Wait!" said Prim, fear in his voice.

"It's alright. Whatever it was, it is gone now." He opened the door, and stepped out into the dying light of the day. The streets were empty still, but when Belknap knelt down, he shuddered at what he saw.

That the markings were tracks was unmistakable. They could not be numbered, such did they spill over each other. But that wasn't what scared Belknap the most. It was what made the tracks that chilled him. Or, should I say, the fact that he had no idea what made them, that he'd never known anything like them before in all his days in the forests that surrounded Arkham.

"Look!"

Belknap followed Prim's shaking finger. The mist rolled on away from them, down the road. Belknap marveled at it, this dark miracle. It was a wall of black cloud. Sheer, like it was made of stone. And just as impenetrable. It crept away from them, as the last light of the sun died away. Belknap's mouth fell open. Of all the things he had seen, it was the unnatural luster of the mist—the cold, green glow that brightened as the night descended—that bothered him most.

"Get McBride," Belknap said over his shoulder, not taking his eyes from the cloud. "The mist moves toward the College. I shall follow it thence. Meet me there."

"Follow it?"

"Go!"

Prim went, and Belknap took one tentative step after another toward the wall of cloud. And with each of those steps, the mist seemed to move one more step away. That is, until it reached Miskatonic. There, it stopped, settled, swallowed the school whole. Belknap came to within ten feet. He would go no further, could go no further. His feet refused to take him one more step. There he waited for Prim to return with McBride, his friend and the village constable. What he saw and what he heard while he waited would haunt him until his dying day.

He had known that something walked within the mist. Now, he heard it. He heard *them*. Mutterings in some unknown tongue. Shrieks, pain-filled and horror-born. Chittering laughter that no human voice could make. But what his ears could hear, his eyes could not perceive; the fog flowed like smoke, and the wind that whipped around Belknap did not move it. It was solid, like marble. But it did show some things.

Flashes of pallid red light outlining shadowed forms, beasts perhaps, but of no kind Belknap knew, and possessing an unsettling and distinctive hint of humanity. And glowing pinpricks. Eyes, Belknap thought. Thousands of eyes. Yet Belknap knew, knew without doubt in that way men know things even when they shouldn't, that only one mind controlled them.

"God in Heaven," said a quavering voice. Belknap turned to see Prim, returned with McBride. "What devilry…"

A crackling interrupted him. A flash, and the cloud turned orange red as if it burned. Then the sound.

Each man heard something different. Prim fell to his knees, clutching his ears and wailing in pain. McBride's face went slack, his mouth moving, and Belknap believed that McBride whispered but a single word—Sara, the name of his wife, dead that summer of the fever.

At first, Belknap heard nothing. Nothing but the sound of the wind blowing, Prim's cries, and McBride's tears. Then in one mad moment, true silence crashed upon him. Leaves rolled along the ground, but made no noise. He could see Prim wail, but could not hear it. McBride shed quiet tears. Had he been struck deaf? Then he heard the voice, and he wished he were deaf, for it said the most terrifying word of them all—his own name.

"Arthur..." It called to him, and he felt himself drawn. If he'd had a rope around his waist, drawing him into the void, the pull would have been no more irresistible. Belknap took a stumbling step forward, then another. "Arthur!" said the voice, louder, urging. Without warning, he stood mere inches from the solid mass of cloud. He could not hear Prim and McBride calling for him, broken from their trances but unwilling to take one step closer to the fog to pull him back. Belknap reached out a hand. One finger extended. He touched the face of the cloud. Only then did he realize what he'd done.

Crimson light flashed, and the world shifted. Belknap no longer stood upon a cobbled street of his native Arkham, but upon a beach he did not know, did not wish to know. The sea lay dead, stinking. Belknap retched, vomited onto the moving sand. The beach teamed with flies, worms, maggots, the foot soldiers of death. He stumbled backward, slamming into a wall of stone. But Belknap was not alone. At the edge of the unmoving sea stood a line of figures, black cloaks spilling down their bodies to the writhing ground. Belknap could not see their faces, did not want to see their faces, and if one had turned to him then, he'd have torn out his eyes before he would look upon it. But they did not turn. Their gaze, he knew, was to the heavens.

Above him, the horned moon held three stars within its sway, three great globes of light that moved inexorably toward one another. Belknap waited, frozen to the spot in terror and fear. The world held its breath. The stars moved. Then they touched, and fire fell from the sky, striking the sea. It boiled. From the depths came a roar, and the ocean erupted. A thousand black cables burst from below, writhing and snapping and slapping the churning water. Then the great beast breached the surface, and Belknap screamed.

The next instant, he found himself staring into Prim's wild eyes set deep in a too pale face. Belknap started and fell backward.

"Arthur, it's alright!" There was a confidence in McBride's voice that calmed him, as did the musket he held in his hands. "Look!"

His eyes followed where his friend pointed, and the buildings of Miskatonic College met his gaze. The cloud was gone.

"What happened?"

"You fell into a sickness," said Prim. "Thrashed about as if a man was shaking you. Then there was a scream from within the mist, and it…vanished."

"It did not vanish," said McBride. "A great wind came upon us, lifted it up into the sky and ripped it apart, like a ship's sail in a gale."

Miskatonic sat silent. A shared question, unspoken, lay before them.

"We should make sure everyone is alright," said Belknap, answering for all. The other men said nothing, but when Belknap stepped beyond the invisible barrier—what had been the limit of the wall of mist—the other men followed.

They found not a soul. Not at first. In fact everything was as should be expected. And yet, in the light of the full moon, nothing stirred. Until a door opened and an elderly man Belknap knew as Reverend Elkanah stumbled out.

"Well," he said, relief flooding his voice, "bless you boys for coming to help."

Belknap spared a glance at McBride, who said, "What happened here, Reverend?"

The elderly man regarded them queerly. "Why, the storm, of course."

"The storm?"

"Yes," he said, looking at each, "one of the most violent I have ever experienced. It must have been a dozen times I thought I'd meet the Lord before it ended. But when it did, suddenly I must say, I knew that I should check on the boys."

More doors opened, more of the teachers and masters who lived on the campus joined the Reverend, and each told the same tale. A terrible storm, powerful gales, fierce lighting and thunder that boomed before the flash even faded. Surely, they all said, the men had experienced the same? The three didn't dare deny it, lest the sanity of all come into question. Instead, they urged the men to their stated goal—to check on the students.

It shouldn't have been a difficult task. There were only twenty boys, and they lived in a handful of cottages along what would become the old yard.

Some of what Belknap relates here strains credulity, echoing as it does some of the more outrageous gothic legends. Dinner, sitting ready on tables. Boiling water on stoves. Tea in cups, still hot.

But whatever is exaggeration and whatever truth, they did not find the boys. Soon they had searched every building on campus. All, save one. Huntington Library.

They saved it for last. Maybe because it seemed the least likely. Maybe because it was big and they knew it would take time to clear. Or maybe they just had one of those feelings.

At any rate, they soon came to the great doors of the library, the three men from town and Elkanah. They waited, in silence, none willing to make the first move. Only Belknap. He stepped forward. He grasped steel rings and pulled. As the smell hit them, Prim vomited; the stench of death filled the air. And what seemed the patter of rain gently falling filled their ears. Belknap's eyes went upward, following the sound.

When he saw it, he didn't gasp. For he could not fully comprehend it, the thing that hung above him, suspended by ropes stained crimson, same as the mass they held. Red. All red.

They'd found one of the students. They never did find his skin.

His body hung from the rafters above the antechamber, tied to the wooden beams that supported the ceiling. Belknap briefly considered how he got there, but there was no time to unravel the mystery. More horror was to come.

"We should get more men," said McBride, and the single musket he bore suddenly seemed woefully insignificant.

"No," Belknap answered. "No, let's see this through." If the other men disagreed, they did not say.

Belknap pulled open the doors of the library itself, a drop of blood splashing onto his hand. Ignoring it, he and the others stepped quickly into the great hall.

They were everywhere, the bodies. All of them horribly disfigured. Mounds of broken bones and flesh, drowning in crimson pools. Belknap was beyond shock now, so horrible were the things he'd already seen. It struck him that one might not even know they were bodies, if there were anything else they could be. The acrid, coppery smell of blood hung as thick in the air as the fog had an hour before.

From one mound to another they walked, and with each one, Prim said a single word, a number. Two and three were on either side of the inner doors. Four through ten were between the first and second fireplaces, both of which burned down to embers. Seven more were on the other side of the great room, in roughly the same places as the ones before them. And eighteen and nineteen were against the far wall. Belknap had the shuddering sensation that could he view the room from a higher vantage, he would recognize a pattern.

"There are only nineteen."

The three men turned and looked at Prim.

"What?" said McBride.

"There are only nineteen...bodies. There are twenty students."

Now every man counted. And every man came to the same number, one short of a score.

"Then where is the twentieth?"

"Perhaps he killed the others and fled?"

Belknap shook his head. "No. One man could not do this."

"But there's nowhere else to look."

"There is." The others turned to Reverend Elkanah. "There is one other chamber, a chamber we never enter, nor do we allow the students to know of its existence."

"Why not?"

"It is foul, ungodly. Cursed, perhaps. When the building was constructed, so too was it made."

"Why don't you just tear it down?"

"Because," said the reverend, "it is underneath us."

Belknap visibly shuddered. This was too much, even for him. But he knew that he would enter the chamber on that day, no matter what the cost.

"Show us, then," said McBride.

Reverend Elkanah led, and the other men followed. They came to the center of the room, around which, Belknap realized, the bodies were arrayed. The floor there was wooden, while the rest had been stone. Elkanah removed a brass key ring from his pocket. He bent down, and then with a quickness that belied his age, stumbled backward.

"What is it?"

"It is unlocked," he said, "and it is covered in blood."

Belknap knelt down and looked. The old man was right. The locking mechanism had been disengaged, the iron ring that served to open this cellar door sticky with red ichor.

He pulled a rag from his pocket, wrapping it around the ring. He looked up at the three men above him, seeking, without words, an acknowledgement that they were ready. And without words, they gave it. Belknap grasped the ring and lifted. The door came away, silent. The scene it revealed was not pitch black, as he expected. Instead, the flicker of soft candlelight met his eyes.

Belknap led the way down the stone stairway. But the horrors above but foreshadowed the horrors below. The candles were many, yet they gave little light. Belknap records that it was as if the darkness was thicker, as if it swallowed the light instead of fleeing from it. And yet even in that pale glow, the scene was laid bare before him.

Something was written on the floor in white chalk. A design, curves bisected by lines that formed sharp angles, doubling back on each other to create the illusion of three dimensions. Triangles surrounding lidless eyes, circles inlaid upon circles. And writing, if you could call it that, though neither the letters nor the words they formed were like anything Belknap had seen before. And at the center of it all, what was left of a body.

He was not a formless lump of flesh like the others. His fate had been different. He had been eviscerated, and his entrails were spread from one corner of the chamber to the other. Split from groin to chest, but the rest of him left intact. His eyes were wide, the glassy orbs staring somewhere beyond, the last horror of what they saw burned into them. Belknap reached down to close them. It was as he brought his hand to the poor boy's face that the youth reached up and grabbed him. And then, in one last burst of life before death finally gave him peace, he said, through the dying rattle of his final breath, these words—

"Do not call up that which you cannot put down!"

Seeing the Wendigo

I was, if you don't mind me sayin', not much older than you, I guess. Maybe even younger, by the look of you. I was a fur man by trade, as my father was before me, and his father before him, all the way back to when my ancestors came from the old country. Huguenots, they were. Fled from one persecution to the next. I guess it was only fitting they should find a home in the woods and the wilds.

This was to be my first time on my own, without my father. You may not know this, but a fur man never travels alone. We work in teams, you see. Trackers and trappers, a man who is handy with a pot and some pans and, if he is worth anything, a hammer and saw. Even a doctor if, per chance, we could find one.

I was in Monterey in those days, a wild bit of country in the Birkshires. There were to be five of us on that trip. The leader was Tom, a big man who looked like he was cut from marble. Tom was a friend of my father's from back in their wilder days, and he had agreed to take me on that trip as his apprentice.

Then there was Dr. Samuels. We never knew if he was a real doc or not, but he had a reputation in the hill country as a man who could be counted on and knew how to treat a fever or a sickness. And, he could fix a wagon. We hauled one behind us as we went. We'd skin the animals as we caught them and, then, line that thing with as many pelts as we could carry. Once the supplies ran out and the wagon was full, we'd make our way back to the outposts along the rivers. But that was always the worst part of the trip. Wheel would break, wagon would get stuck. Without a man who knew his way around some carpentry, we would be lost. I had some of that knowledge, but the doc was the best with a knife, whether he was cutting on a man or a pine board.

Andrew was another trapper; skinny fellow, that one. He struck me as a bit skittish straightaway, and I marked him as a man you couldn't trust. Joe was our scout. He was a bit of a mystery. He was a tracker by trade, though he could probably trap better than the rest of us, too. They said he was part Indian; I never learned the truth of that. He died too soon. And, he was quiet. Spoke barely a word.

And, then there was Travis. Travis was an experienced hand. He knew the woods, knew the secret paths, the dark places where the best fur would hide. There was something about that man, something missing from his eyes. I know that sounds strange. But that's what I felt. Like he was empty somehow. But Tom wanted him. Between Tom and Andrew, Travis, and me, we had a pretty good team goin'. There were no doubts we would make good coin on that trip. And, so I guess we got a little wild, as men like us were wont to do. On the night before we were supposed to leave, the wine, the whiskey, and the rum flowed hard and fast.

Tom had a rule on the trail—no liquor, no exceptions. It bein' the last night in town, I guess we drank a little more than we should. There was a girl who worked the bar that evening, an Indian girl. Travis watched her all night long. She was shy and a tiny bit of nothin'. Dark haired and dark skinned. Young, no more than 16, I'd wager. Every time she'd walk by, Travis would grab her, pull her to him, tell her she was "a pretty little thing."

It boils my blood to even think about it. There was a sickness in his voice then, a nasty, godless quality. Depraved, he was. Just depraved.

Anyway, she obliged him at first, as any good girl in that trade would. But then it was too much even for someone who made her money off men like Travis. She began to struggle, to try and get away. Andy told him—that's what we called Andrew—Andy told him to leave her alone. Travis just glared at him. He scared me, then, with that look. I wanted no part of that.

I left the bar and found Tom outside, smoking his tobacco.

There was the hint of coming snow that day, but it wasn't cold.

"You ready for tomorrow?" he asked between puffs. I wasn't really sure. I had only gone with my father before, never with anyone I didn't know.

"Sure, I am," I said, mustering as much confidence in my voice as I could manage.

"Good, I'm going to need you," he said. He didn't say how or why. I simply nodded. I had learned not to question men like Tom too often, and then to ask only the questions that really needed answerin'. But I'd be lyin' if I didn't say there was something about that night that scared me. I don't know how I knew it then, but the trip already felt foul, as if it was marked from the beginning.

I stumbled through the darkness, the haze of the whiskey thick on my brain. I don't know how long passed before I found my way to my bunk, but I do know my head had barely hit the pillow when I was asleep.

I had strange dreams that night, nightmares filled with flashes of light and thunder. I was in the forest, but I was alone. I still remember, even as I was dreaming, that I was struck by my own loneliness. "Never trap alone." That was my father's cardinal rule. But there I was, without another soul in sight. It was a familiar forest, and I felt I knew it, but in that familiarity there was also great fear, as if something wasn't quite right. The forest was like Travis's eyes. It was missing something, something basic and good. It was quiet, too. A stillness as unnatural as it was complete. Nothing moved there. Nothing.

And, then it was night. I can't explain it, but just as suddenly as you could strike a match, the sun vanished from the sky. Darkness and silence. Isolation, loneliness. Those were the things that overwhelmed me. But there was a voice in my head, too, the voice of my father.

"Steady on, Jack, steady on. You have a job to do. If you don't finish it, no one will."

And, so I began to move. But then came the thunder. Then, came the light. It roared and flashed throughout the wood, and it was all the more horrible because of the silence it shattered. Then a single roar over all others—the screeching of a bird, a great and terrible beast unlike any flying thing you ever saw. A great black shadow covered me so thick even the flashes of lightening couldn't lift it.

I woke, then, drenched in sweat, screaming. I sat bolt upright in my bed. Joe was sitting across from me, just a-starin', his black Indian eyes just as impenetrable as the meaning of my dream.

"What did you see?" he asked. If he had spoken a word to me before that moment, it's not one I remember.

"Nothin'. Just a dream," I said.

"No dream. What did you see?" he asked again, this time more forcefully. He had me scared, then, but I wasn't going to relive that, no matter what he did.

So I just said, "I told you, nothin'."

I'm old enough now to know something I didn't know then—an angry man, or a scared man, he's liable to turn in a moment. To snap, as they say. And, Joe snapped then. He leapt from his bunk clear across the room to mine and grabbed me around the throat. His mouth made sounds, but if they were words I could understand, I sure as Hell didn't then. I think he would have killed me. Well, I damn sure know he would have killed me, but then I felt him fly away from me. I looked up and through my near-on blacked out eyes I saw Tom sling Joe across the room like he was a bag of dirty laundry.

"Enough!" I remember he thundered like Zeus himself. "You two get your gear. We've already overstayed our welcome here."

There was anger in his face, but I knew despite my youth that it wasn't directed at us. He stood there for a moment longer and, then, turned to go, saying, "Be at the wagon in five minutes."

Three minutes later I emerged into the morning sun. Tom was at the wagon with Dr. Samuels loading the last bit of supplies. Travis was there, too, sitting on the buckboard smoking a rolled cigar. He was smirking, and like everything else Travis did, there was no joy there. Just a cruel, cold sneer. Joe and I walked over together, but I kept my distance. Whatever had come over him earlier, now he was as implacable as the grave. That same flat, stone-faced look I guess he always wore. I could see Tom and Travis were talking, and I could tell it wasn't a pleasant conversation.

"Damn it, Travis!" I heard him say. "You're bringing bad luck on us, bad luck already."

I heard Travis curse in response. "I make my own luck, Captain," he growled in that flat, toneless voice of his. Where he was from, I didn't know, and his voice didn't betray it, either. I just knew it was a place I didn't want to visit.

"That's right, Travis, you do," Tom replied. "And, that's the fear, isn't it?"

I didn't know what they were on about, but I was sure it had something to do with Tom's sudden desire to get out of that place as soon as he could. I loaded up my gear in silence and climbed aboard. Joe and the doc followed. Andy skulked about, doing his best to stay invisible. It was his way, I guess. Tom had the reins of the horses, and we were about to leave. I suppose, if we had been a little quicker, I might not be sitting here today. But that's the way of the world, right? For just as Tom was about to lead us out of that place, there was a shriek, a howl really, that stopped us dead in our tracks. Then, it turned to a word.

"You!" it bellowed. We turned as one, turned and saw an old Indian woman, older than I am now I would suppose. She had that little girl from the pub by the arm and was dragging her along behind her. But she wasn't pretty then, probably wouldn't be pretty for a long time after that. Her face was shattered. That's about the only way to put it. Her lips were busted, and her cheeks bruised. One eye was so swollen she couldn't have opened it for King Phillip himself. She was crying, though. I guess that must have hurt quite a bit.

I gaped at her, mouth as open as it could be. I had never seen nothing like it. I followed the old woman's eyes to Travis. He didn't look shocked. He just sat there and smiled, smiled that same awful smirk he always had. This was nothing to him. Tom just looked from the woman to Travis and, then, struck the horses. He didn't take his eyes off of the road until we were clear out of town. But the woman didn't stop. She dragged that girl until they were running alongside the wagon.

"You did this!" she screamed at Travis in a thickly veiled tongue I could barely understand. Travis just smiled even broader and shrugged his shoulders. Then, the woman threw the girl to the ground and pointed at Travis. I couldn't understand some of what she said, and I have come to believe that most of it wasn't English. In her ravings and cryings, I only really caught a couple words.

Curse. And *Wendigo*.

Travis chuckled. And, that was it. The wagon rolled along, and we sat in silence except for the creaking of the wheels and the crinkling of the tobacco in Travis's cigar as his breath ignited it. I looked around the wagon. Tom was emotionless. Doc Stanley was not as disciplined a man, and if Travis had cared to look he would have seen a snarl of disgust on his face. Andy just looked scared. But it was Joe that interested me the most. He looked off through the forest, peering really, and mumbled to himself.

Despite our earlier encounter, my curiosity got the better of me. I reached across the wagon and tapped Joe on the shoulder. He spun around, and when he looked at me, I knew the face of terror.

His skin was ashen, his dark hair drenched with sweat. The eyes were the worst, though. They were opened wide, pupils as big as saucers. And, on he mumbled. He grabbed me on the shoulders.

"He will come for us now!" he screamed. It was as if he had gone mad. Out of the corner of my eye, I saw movement. Travis landed a swift kick right to Joe's midsection.

"Shut it, you damn fool," he spat. "Superstitious bullshit, that is. There ain't nothing out here but what we're gonna kill. Should have left you behind with the rest of your kind."

"Silence!" Tom yelled, the veins in his neck beginning to throb. "One day in, and I don't need this!"

Travis leaned back and returned to his cigar. Joe just rocked back and forth on the floor of the wagon, while Andy looked the worst of the group. We rumbled along, deeper into the woods. We didn't stop till night fall, not that day. When I felt it was safe to speak, I moved quietly over to Andy who still looked as though the fear of God was in him.

"You alright?" I asked.

"No," Andy spat. "And, you ain't either. You're just too stupid to know it."

I let it pass. "What's wrong? What was Joe all up about?"

Andy looked at me with terror-filled eyes and said, "The Wendigo."

* * *

For the second time that day I heard a word that had never met my ears in my previous 18 years of life.

"What," I began to ask, swallowing deeply before I continued, "is the Wendigo?"

The voice that answered me was not Andy's. It was deeper, stronger. I turned to see Joe had pulled himself up and leaned against the side of the wagon. Whatever panic had covered him before now seemed to vanish as he spoke. His voice was melodic. On the surface it was steady and firm, but I sensed the fear still lurking beneath its seemingly calm waters.

"The Wendigo," he began, "is the whisper in the darkness, the voice in the night. He is the wind that shakes the forest, the thunder in the blizzard, the lightening flash that follows. The Wendigo is death."

Andy whimpered audibly and then curled himself into a tightly wound ball. I looked from him back to Joe's now-bloodless face. Then Doc Stanley interrupted.

"All superstition and myth," he said. "None of it's true." He cut his eyes to Joe and in that look there was a none-too-subtle command to end this talk now. The forest is no place to lose your head. Joe, however, did not keep his peace.

"No myth," he said. "Long ago, before the age of man, there walked this Earth a race whose name is now lost to us, if it was ever known. My people speak of them. These are the Great Old Ones, creatures of legend who for eons ruled the forests and the plains, the sea and even the sky from whence they came. Some say they were gods, but I do not believe it. They were cruel and cold-hearted. They reveled in pain and their hearts were filled with hate. The world was covered in darkness then, and if men had been there to see their cruelty, the agony of it would still be burned into our memory, even now.

"There was one who ruled over them all, one who made them

and formed them. We do not speak his name, and I will not speak it here. The Old Ones were his spawn, and thousands they were, but he loved one above all others—a daughter, Lilitu. Lilitu was as beautiful as she was depraved. She gave herself freely to her brothers, the sons of the dark one. But unto one of her kin, Witiko, he who lusted for her most fiercely, she refused. As his desire burned within him, Lilitu mocked Witiko until finally he took her by force. But it was all part of her ploy, you see, all part of her game. She went to her father and cried out for his vengeance on Witiko. In a mockery of all that is holy, Witiko was brought before his father to face his 'justice.' Witiko was not killed. Instead he was stripped of his authority and power on this Earth, stripped even of his name.

"'You shall be Wendigo,' his father roared. 'You shall walk the Earth alone. Off it you shall gain no sustenance. You shall eat of neither the plants of the forest nor the plain, nor of the animals that now swarm about us. Pain will be all that you know.'

"And so the Wendigo was banished from his brethren, and in pain and darkness he traveled the land, his skin stretched tight over his bones, his hunger burning as bright as his hate. But the age of the Old Ones passed, and only the Wendigo remained. A new creature arose then, one that had not been refused to the Wendigo, one unknown to his father. This was man, and he the Wendigo could eat. Since then, the Wendigo has haunted the north woods, devouring whomever he finds as prey. From him, the Wendigo takes his knowledge and his skill, but never gains sustenance, never fills his hunger, never quenches his hate. This is the Wendigo, and now, he comes for us."

"Bah!" Doc Stanley spat. "No more of this! There is no Wendigo."

"What of the stories then?" Andy muttered through his creeping fear.

"A disease of the mind," the doctor responded matter-of-factly.

"Wait," I said, breaking my silence for the first time, "you mean to tell me there is some truth to this?" Until that moment, Joe's ravings, though frightening in their power, struck me as nothing more than a myth from the old days. But now the doctor appeared to give them some weight.

"Well," the doctor replied, stuttering, "the legend, such that it is—absurdities all, of course—is not merely that the Wendigo devours his victims. You see…" He paused then, studying his hands. It gave me no calm that the doctor seemed to give more than a little credence to the story. "Oh, it's rubbish. We shouldn't talk any more of this."

"He takes you," Joe interjected. "His spirit is strong, stronger than yours. But his body was imprisoned long ago, along with all the Old Ones. They speak to us only in dreams now. But the curse gave the Wendigo power beyond even theirs. But though he lives, he must take the form of a man to partake of this world. Whomever he takes is doomed to feast upon the flesh of his brothers, to watch through eyes that are no longer his as the Wendigo devours all before him."

"It's a mental defect," the doctor spat, showing both his own frustration but also a hint of doubt. "Certain of the Indian tribes around these parts are known to succumb to it. To explain their sudden insanity and…cannibalism, the legend of the Wendigo was invented. That is all. These are mad men and nothing more. And if you persist in this kind of talk, we are liable to lose our own minds over these next few months."

I suppose it might have gone on like that for a few more hours, but at that moment Tom pulled the wagon to a stop. We had arrived at the first of our campsites. The next few hours of work made us forget quickly about the curse that had been laid upon us, about the Wendigo. But as I lay in my tent that night, I couldn't help but hear whispers on the wind as the first snows of winter began to fall in earnest.

* * *

Without notice our duties consumed us. The life of the men of the forest is not one of leisure. As the air grew colder, the work got harder. I was used to a more lenient taskmaster—my father. But Tom was relentless. He was the best in the western woods, that's certain. But there was a growing gloom above us as well, and as the moon waxed brighter, as a steel-gray curtain of clouds rose, and as the icy cold wind cut through our tents and our clothes, it was clear to all that the season's worst was near.

"A storm's a-comin'," I remember Joe saying. It was prescient, I suppose, but it didn't take his particular senses to know a blizzard was upon us. Tom was worried, too.

"We should close up early tonight," he said. He had a wary eye on the dim light of the setting sun. It was an hour yet until twilight, but thick clouds had rendered it night already. "Everyone, make sure everything is double secure tonight. Trust me when I say night in a snowstorm is no time to try and pitch a tent."

Tom's point was well taken, but it was advice we didn't need. We had already begun the work and were well underway before the first burst of snow. Joe was our cook, but he had a hard time getting anything together that night. The winds and the snow were such that the fire would barely stay lit, no matter how much wood we fed it.

We bedded down early. I stood at the opening of my tent and watched as the snow began to fall in ever greater quantities. I glanced back at the dying fire and saw Joe still sat at its edge. The waning embers did not give much light, but he had drawn near to their warmth, and the rays that remained illuminated his face. Perhaps it was the light or the shadow or the snow, but I noticed for the first time that Joe had aged over the past few weeks. The lines were deeper, the skin more leathery and pulled taut across his face. His eyes were simply empty. There was no fear, no worry, just nothing, a cold resignation that frightened me more than anything else possibly could. That may sound strange, but I know no other way to describe it.

They say man is an animal, and that may be so. But most men don't know nature. They are like you, my young friend. They live in the world of the city, and when they come to the wild it is for leisure and peace. They do not see the cold killer lurking in the darkness, the hunter red in tooth and claw. But we saw it that night.

The blizzard came hard and fast, falling upon us like the eagle strikes its prey. I lay listening as the wind buffeted my tent, and the snow struck its sides like grapeshot fired from a distant cannon. I know I slept that night, as strange and unbelievable as it might sound. Yes, the work had exhausted me, but my senses were so heightened, my fear so deep, that sleep should never have come. I was as a man taken by opium, and my eyes grew heavy, my mind grew cloudy, and I drifted in and out of consciousness.

I cannot know how much of what I remember was real or imagined. But I heard things that night. Not just the wind or the snow. It started with a howl, a low and distant whine. I wasn't sure it was there at first, thought it might just be something from a dream. Soon it was joined by another and another. It was as if all the wolves in the western wood had suddenly been called to a common purpose.

But it wasn't the howl itself that sent a chill through my bones. No, it was the message of that call. It was pain and fear from an animal that rarely knew either. At one moment the sound was all about, as if we were surrounded. Then just as quickly it seemed to be coming from within my own mind. And then it changed, my God, did it change. No more the call of a wild dog. Now it was the pitiful cry of a woman. So deep was her anguish, so terrible. As if the world had been taken from her, as if a child had been ripped from her bosom and slaughtered before her very eyes. Oh, the pain in that cry. But it was not the worst I heard, no, not at all. Vile sounds followed, sounds that are beyond my meager education to describe, but I wager the greatest poet in the world couldn't write a line for them. Demon haunted the forest was that night, and in my dreams, I heard and felt the darkest and foulest beast that ever gibbered its wail from the depths of the pit.

There was thunder that followed lightening, the mark of a summer storm in the heart of winter. In those flashes of light, I saw figures outlined against the thin skin of my tent, figures that danced outside my vision. And then, even in the night, even in the darkness, a shadow fell upon me, that of a great bird, a flying beast never before seen on this Earth by the eyes of man. Its cry rent the night air, and in that moment my mind snapped, and I sunk into blessed black oblivion.

* * *

I awoke the next morning to the brilliant, blinding light of the morning sun shining through my now open tent. Outlined in its gleam was Doc Stanley. If the bitter night had shaken him, the blank expression on his face did little to reveal it.

"Get up," he commanded. "Joe is missing." And with that, he turned and was gone.

I pulled on boots and rushed outside to find the entire campsite covered in snow. I remembered the wolves and immediately walked around to the back of my tent. I expected to find paw prints, fur, something. But there was only snow, thick and as untouched as a lamb that had never been sheered. I told myself it had been all a dream or that, at worst, the snow had covered whatever markings the beasts had left behind. I told myself that, but even in those early days I didn't believe it.

Then I heard my name. It was Tom. I walked back to the center of the campsite to find the entire group gathered around the spot where the fire had been before. Tom was serious, Doc Stanley's expression remained as impenetrable as the grave, and Andy looked like he wanted to crawl into a hole and hide. Travis merely seemed irritated.

"What's going on?" I asked.

Tom sighed and said, "Joe is gone. He should have been up making breakfast by now, but as you can probably see, he never even started the fire."

"Maybe he needed some wood," I offered.

"We cut some yesterday," Doc Stanley replied. I knew this. I had helped break it up.

"Maybe something was wrong with it." Tom sighed again, and I saw Doc cast a weary look his way. When Tom didn't speak, Doc Stanley did.

"He didn't go for wood," Stanley said. "His tent is empty, and there are no footprints. No footprints anywhere. Not going to it, not going away. Nothing. It's like..." Andy whimpered, and for a second Doc Stanley paused. He looked at him with less contempt than I expected and then said, "It's like Joe disappeared. Just up and vanished. We looked in his tent. Everything is in place. Nothing messed up, nothing broken. And, nothing taken. It looks like he just walked out of camp with nothing but the clothes on his back."

"Oh, God," Andy stammered, "Joe knew this trip was trouble. Knew it was trouble from the start. And, now it's got him."

Doc Stanley jerked his head toward Andy and fixed him with one of the most hate-filled gazes I've ever seen.

"Who's got him?" Tom asked.

"The Wendigo!" Andy cried, oblivious to Doc Stanley.

"Oh, not this rubbish," Doc Stanley said as he turned and walked toward his tent.

"Look." Now it was Travis's time to talk. "Ain't nobody here who put any stock in Joe. I don't even know why you brought him along," he spat, pointing a long narrow finger at Tom. "He was always liable to run off, and now he has. He probably left last night. He probably got spooked by the storm and struck off into the woods. The snow covered his tracks, and he's gone. If the wolves haven't gotten him, the snow damn sure did. He's probably buried under three feet of it now."

"You heard the wolves too?" I asked.

Travis's eyes went from mine to Tom's, and as I followed them I saw the answer to my question in both their faces.

"No, kid," Travis lied. "I was just sayin' is all. There ain't no wolves in these parts. But Joe is dead either way."

Tom still hadn't spoken, and I knew given how he guarded his words, he wasn't likely to.

Then Travis continued. "Look, we got dry wood. You clean off a spot," he said to me, "and I'll get a fire going. I think I can round up something for us to eat. And, then we can go look for Joe."

When I heard that I lost my words. Travis didn't do anything for anybody, had never made food for us. Now Tom did speak. "You don't cook," he said.

"Yeah, well, looks like somebody has to learn, huh?"

With that he turned and walked away. I went to work clearing a spot for a fire, and soon we had a pretty big one going. Before the sun had risen too far in the sky, Travis had cooked up some of the rabbit we had trapped the day before. For a man who had no way with food, I remember thinking to myself that it wasn't half bad. I had never thought much of Joe's cooking, and I reckoned what Travis had made was just as good. I ate more than I was accustomed to. I was hungry, and Travis, though he had cooked it himself, obviously had doubts about his ability as he ate almost none.

"Not hungry this mornin'," he said. Something with his stomach.

We ate quickly. If Joe were still alive out there, we needed to find him and find him fast. Tom gave us our orders.

"Each man take a line and walk it. Don't wander off. We'll cover the forest close by as good as we can, but I don't want nobody else gettin' lost. You walk straight out and then you follow your tracks and come straight back. You got it?"

Each man nodded his assent, and we were off. Before long, the camp was far behind me, and I could no longer see the man to either my right or left. The forest was thick, and if Joe had climbed under a bush or a tree for cover in the storm, there would be no finding him now. With the snow as thick as it was, I doubted I would spot him unless I damn near stepped on his chest. I began to think back to the night before, the things I had heard, seen. The thought of it made me stop in my tracks. If any of it were real, even a fraction of it, then Joe would never have left his tent. Never willingly, that is. No man would, and especially not one as superstitious as he. Joe was no coward; I would never claim that. But I wouldn't call it courage that would lead a man to have stepped into that maelstrom. And, that could mean only one thing—someone had taken him. Someone big—Joe was a strong man. His attacker had done it without making a sound, without knocking a single thing out of place, without leaving any evidence of his having been there.

The forest changed. I noticed every sound, every twig snapping, every creak of every tree. Something, and I didn't know what it was, was out there, and suddenly I felt the cold stare of an unknown pair of eyes on me. I spun around, peering into the blinding white wilderness that surrounded me. That's when I saw Joe.

He was standing a couple hundred yards from me. His arms and legs were spread wide, like he was trying to hold up the two trees on either side of him, or like he was trying to hug the world.

His mouth was slightly open, his head cocked to the left. He was completely naked. At first, I didn't know what to do. He had clearly lost his mind, and I knew he must be freezing. But I started toward him anyway. He was alive, and I would do my best to save him.

But as I walked toward him he never moved, even though I knew he had to see me. Then I began to notice something was wrong. Joe was a big man, but he didn't look big anymore. He looked thin. He looked small. He looked…empty. Then I saw the ropes, one tied around each hand and each foot. They ran to the trees on either side, and there was another rope running to the branch above his head. I recognized the purpose immediately and wished I could not. I had done it a thousand times. Each time I had stripped a raccoon and laid out its hide to tan the pelt. At that moment I saw the blood, the pool that dripped down from the seams where Joe's skin had been ripped from his body.

I didn't scream. I just turned and ran. I ran blindly. I smashed through branches, slashing my cheek so deeply the blood flowed down my face. I fell no less than three times, but by some miracle I found myself back at the camp.

Tom was the only one there, and I quickly fell at his feet. He looked at me like I had lost my mind, and part of me wondered if I had. He grabbed me by the shoulders and pulled me up.

"What's the meaning of this, boy?" he screamed in my face. There was fear in his eyes, and that was an emotion you didn't often see from him.

"It's Joe," I said through gulps of breath. "I found him."

"Then why didn't you bring him back?"

"He's sliced up," I remember saying. "Skinned like an animal."

"Skinned?" Tom whispered. The anger and excitement had vanished from his voice. He didn't know if he should believe me, but he had no doubt he didn't want to. "Show me," he commanded.

I led him, reluctantly I might add, back down the path made by my boots in the snow. It had seemed so far before, and now my fevered mind wanted nothing more than to never reach my destination, yet it came more quickly than seemed possible. Then we arrived, and the thing I feared most to see met my eyes. There was no body. But fortunately, if you can use that word, the once pure white snow was stained a dark crimson red. Tom stepped forward and knelt down where the red snow began. He then looked at me.

"So the body was here?" he asked.

"Yes."

"Only a few minutes before?"

"Yes."

"Then, where is it now?"

"I don't know."

Tom sighed deeply and stood up.

"Well," he said calmly but to no one in particular, "it was definitely here before." He turned back to me. "You sure it was Joe? You sure it wasn't just an animal?"

"He wasn't just lying there. He was tied up to the tree. He was tied up like you'd tan a hide. He was here, Tom. He was here, and now he's gone, and that means somebody took him. Ain't no animal done this."

"No," Tom said decisively. "No animal did it. And, that means we are all in danger here. Let's get back to the camp. With any luck, the others will be there, too." He turned and took a couple steps. Then he stopped. "Look," he said, "it's good enough to tell them that Joe is dead, and someone took his body. That's enough. They don't need to know how you found him."

I nodded my head to show him I understood, and we turned and hurried back to the camp. Tom was in front, and I noticed that he constantly glanced from side to side as we moved along. If whatever had taken Joe was around us, he at least wanted to see him coming. We found Doc Stanley, Andy, and Travis huddled around the fire.

"About damn time," Travis grunted. Tom ignored him.

"Did you find anything?" Andy asked, his voice shaking. I could only imagine how he was going to react to what he was about to hear. Tom ignored him, as well.

"Joe is dead," Tom said matter-of-factly.

"Dead?" Andy stuttered.

"Mountain lion?" Doc Stanley asked nonchalantly.

"No, he was murdered." Tom let his pronouncement sink in.

Doc Stanley went pale while Andy looked like he might pass out. Only Travis kept his cool. "And his body has been taken." Now Andy did fall to his knees. No one seemed to notice.

"Who could have done this?" Doc Stanley asked. "There were no footprints, no signs of struggle."

"The Wendigo," Andy muttered as he rocked back and forth.

"He must have heard something, saw something," Tom answered. "He left camp, and somebody got him. Then, the snow covered his tracks. It's as simple as that. No ghosts. It's a man out there, or men."

"We should hunt 'em down and kill 'em," Travis spat. "I got no love for Joe, but he was one of ours."

"No!" Andy wailed. "We gotta get out of here. No man did this, and we can't kill what did. Let's go. Let's go now!"

Tom waved his hand as if to dismiss him. "We ain't going now, and we ain't going to hunt down who did this. The day's already burnt up. We're going to stay here tonight, and then at first light we start heading back to town. I don't want to hear nothin' else about it. We'll take turns tonight keeping watch. They won't trick us again, and anybody who shows up won't be walkin' out."

"Who's goin' first?" Andy moaned.

"I'll go, I'll take the first watch," Doc Stanley said, casting a contemptuous glance at Andy. "But you will damn well have to do it at some point, by God."

"Right," Tom said. "Jack, can you take second watch?"

"Yah," I muttered. I would say I wasn't scared, but that would be a lie.

"I'll take next, then Travis. And Andy, I think you can handle the last watch till sunrise."

Andy didn't look too confident, but he didn't complain. It was the best he could hope for.

"Good," Tom said, looking to the west. The sun had fallen below the horizon, and soon it would be dark. "I suggest you all get some sleep," he continued. "It's going to be a long night."

* * *

As I walked to my tent, I noticed Doc Stanley pulling a crate close to our fire. He held a rifle in his hand, the same I knew I would have to bear in only a few short hours. I hoped I would not need to use it. He rubbed oil along the stock, and I could tell he was trying desperately to remain calm. I grabbed two logs and walked over to him. As I threw them on the fire, he looked up.

"Thank you, Jack," he said quietly, rubbing a thick rag back and forth along the rifle. I simply nodded and took a seat on the ground next to him. For a moment, I just sat there. He didn't speak, and I didn't know what to say. I couldn't know, of course, what was coming or when it would hit, but I had a feeling that whatever it was, Doc Stanly had the best chance of seeing it first.

Finally he broke the silence. "You should go on," he said. "You won't get much sleep, and there's no telling what you might see."

I simply nodded in reply. But I had a question before I went.

"Doc, I saw Joe. I saw him today out in the woods. Tom didn't want me to say anything, but I saw him, and ain't no man did that. No animal, either."

Doc Stanley held up his hand. "I know," he said simply. "Tom told me about it. Didn't want you to say nothing cause of what it would have done to Andy."

"Then, you know we ain't dealing with nothin' you can kill with that gun?"

He turned and looked at me then, and I saw fear in his face. He knew all too well.

"We survive the night, then we get out of here. He has power in the forest, but not in the cities. He is the lord of a lost world. He draws his strength from the wild."

"He?" I asked stupidly, as if I didn't know.

"The Wendigo," Doc Stanley replied matter-of-factly. "No question of that now."

"But I thought you didn't believe in that?"

"Oh, I believe," he said. "Seen too many things out here not to. You would have come to believe, too, even if this had never happened. But now it has. We are at the mercy of the Old One now, and there is no power we possess that can stop him."

There was a haunting call in the distance, as if to punctuate the doctor's words. I saw his eyes narrow and then, "Whippoorwill," he said. "Bad sign. They should be long gone by now. But they follow death, so I suppose we shouldn't be surprised."

"Is there any way to stop it? The Wendigo I mean?"

"You ever met anybody who has seen the Wendigo?" Doc Stanley asked.

"Well, no," I stammered, "but I had never even heard of it 'til this trip."

The doctor allowed himself a chuckle. "Fair enough. But I will just go ahead and tell you that I've been wandering these woods for thirty years, and I've not met a soul that saw him and came out of it alive. So, I don't suppose there is a way to stop him." Then, he paused. "Of course, the legends do speak of a weakness."

Doc Stanley looked up from his work and furrowed his brow. "They say he was the most beautiful of them all, the Old Ones, but when he was cursed, his beauty was taken, and he was rendered hideous to behold. And, perhaps if you were to show him his own image, you might have a chance. But, like I said, that legend has been around for as long as I can remember, too, yet I've never met a man who used it to his advantage."

I looked out into the now darkening forest, and in my mind's eye I saw the Wendigo in every tree, in every swaying branch, in every rustling bush. "So, he's really out there," I said.

Doc Stanley just smiled.

"There's nothing out there, Jack." I looked at him and didn't understand. After all this, I thought there was no question.

"What do you mean?" I asked. Doc Stanley looked up and off into the distance, and I saw him make a decision.

"You should know," he said, turning to me. "Tom didn't want to tell you, but you should know. The Old Ones have passed from this Earth, at least in their physical form. The Wendigo is a spirit, a powerful one, yes, but not strong enough to act in this world. Not without a body, at least." Doc Stanley looked at me, seeing if I understood. I did not. "The Wendigo, my friend, is one of us."

I sat there a second, not believing what I had heard. Then, I turned slowly, looking back at the tents behind me, wondering about the men who lay within.

"But if it's not you, and it's not me," I began, but Doc Stanley held up his hand to stop me.

"We don't know that is true."

"What?" is all I could manage.

"The curse of the Wendigo is upon us. Whoever he has taken, he will soon take completely. Only the dead are above suspicion. The true horror of the curse is that he who has been chosen does not know it at first. The Great Old Ones are the masters of dreams, and in those dreams they will possess you. To he who is Wendigo, the possession will begin as nothing more than a nightmare, a horrible flash of color and pain. But, eventually, the power of the Wendigo will overcome him, and he will live the life of the undead, locked in his own mind, seeing through his own eyes as he does unspeakable things, but having no power to control it."

I thought back to the night Joe disappeared, to the fevered and demon-haunted dreams that filled my mind. I shuddered, then, at the horror that might be before me.

"So, tonight," Doc Stanley continued, "I will be watching the others. It is not the things of the forest I fear. It is what lurks in our own midst. Now, it is late. Go sleep, if sleep will come."

I left him, then, and something inside of me knew two things: I would not sleep that night, and I would never see Doc Stanley again.

* * *

I didn't sleep. My fevered mind raced from dark thought to darker. It seemed to me there could be only two choices. Either I was the Wendigo or I would die at his hands. That one fate was more horrible than the next offered no comfort. And, that death was the preferable choice... These were the thoughts that filled my mind, and my troubled soul found no respite.

After several hours, I decided there was no point, and I arose to relieve Doc Stanley. The fire still burned, but Stanley was gone. He had not disappeared without a trace; in the flickering firelight, I could see blood dripping from the box on which he had sat. The area around it was stained crimson with the same blood. The rifle lay in the snow. I could see something else was beside it, something that shimmered tan against the red blood beneath it. But I ignored whatever it was. I needed the rifle. That was my primary concern.

I walked quickly to where it lay and offered a glance to the thing that sat beside it. And, then I fell backward. It was Doc Stanley's face—just his face—as if it had been ripped clean from his skull. Empty black holes stared up at me where his eyes should have been.

I reached down and grabbed up the gun. It was still sticky with dried blood. Then I heard quick footsteps behind me. I spun around and shouldered the rifle, but it was only the others. It was then that I realized I had been screaming the whole time.

"What happened here?" Tom yelled.

"I don't know. I just found him like this."

Tom stepped forward and saw the face that still sat upon the ground. He stumbled backward and looked at me. The wind picked up, and in that wind was a voice—that of Doc Stanley.

"Help me!" it cried, begged. Oh, it was a horrible voice, a moaning shriek that rent the air and my soul. We all heard it, each man. We turned about ourselves trying desperately to place it. But it was to our left and, then, our right. It was in front and then behind. Finally it was everywhere, all around, all at once.

"Tell us what happened," Tom commanded above the voice in the wind.

"I've told you. I got up and found this."

"You didn't hear anything? You didn't see anything?"

"No!" I screamed. "Nothing!"

"How is that possible, Jack?" Tom stated more than asked.

"How is any of this possible?" I screamed.

"Give me the gun, Jack," Tom commanded. His voice was too calm, too under control. He was struggling to keep it that way. Then, suddenly I realized—he thought it was me. We stood there in silence for a second as Doc Stanley's wail echoed around us, sometimes louder, sometimes not.

"No!" I shouted, as firmly as my feeble heart could manage.

"That's an order, son," Tom said calmly.

"I think we're beyond orders now, Captain," I replied.

"Enough of this foolishness!" Travis growled, taking a step forward. "Give me the gun!"

I shouldered the rifle and leveled it at Travis's heart.

"I'll shoot any man who tries to take it from me."

"You can't kill us all," Travis spat, taking another step.

"But I can damn sure kill you, Travis Walker. Damn sure. It was you who brought this down on us. Two men are already dead for what you done. And, if I am going to die tonight, you sure as Hell are going with me."

"Look, Jack," Tom said, "it's one of us. You know that. It could be you. Can you live with it if it is?"

"It could be you, too, Tom. You don't know any better than me."

"It was you who found Joe," Travis said. "And you who found the Doc, or what's left of him, at least. You think that was a coincidence?"

I turned back to Travis. "And what about you?" I said. "Never cooked a day in your life, and then Joe dies, and all of a sudden you can? And, I noticed you didn't eat any of it either. Was it 'cause you couldn't?"

"Now, wait one minute," Travis said, backing up and putting a hand out to Tom who was now eying him suspiciously. "I was sick, you know that," he said, pointing at Tom.

"I don't know anything, Travis. All I know is the boy is right."

"And, where were you when we found Joe's body? Huh?" Andy stammered. "We came back to the camp, and you were still gone. It had to be you that took it."

Travis turned to me. His face contorted into a snarl. He took a step toward me. I raised my rifle back at him and started to pull the trigger. But before I could, there was a thud as Tom smashed a piece of firewood against the crown of Travis's skull. His eyes rolled back in his head, and Travis collapsed to the ground.

"Tie him up!" Tom commanded.

We pulled Travis up to the wagon and lashed his hands and feet to its side. It was no easy task. He was all dead weight, and Andy was little help. Eventually he was tied fast. We waited for him to awaken. Only then would we find some answers.

* * *

For many long minutes we stood there, our eyes on Travis's limp body. The fire roared behind us. We had built it up to a blaze, whether to provide light or buoy our sinking spirits, I don't really know.

"So, what do we do with him?" Andy asked. "Maybe we should kill him now."

Tom pursed his lips, thinking on Andy's suggestion. "No," he said, "no, we won't do that. We don't know for sure it's him."

I turned from Travis and stared at Tom. "You don't still suspect me?"

"I don't know who to suspect," Tom answered firmly. "I know what you said about Travis, and that seemed pretty right to me. But we can't know. We just can't know. And, until we do, we can't kill him."

"I hear you, Captain, I really do," I said. "But something tells me, if he is the one, those ropes won't hold him."

No one said anything else. Hours passed, and the night deepened. And, then Travis awoke. It was slow at first. His eyes fluttered, then were filled with confusion. He strained for a second against the bonds that held him, and then he knew. Now he was angry.

"You sons of bitches!" he screamed. "What the Hell are you doing? It's him you want!"

"Is it Travis? Is it?" Tom asked, stepping in front of me. "You're going to talk, and you're going to do it now. These men," he said, gesturing to me and Andy, "they think we should kill you now. I said we wait. But if you don't answer me, I may just let them."

Travis simply spat at Tom; it was his way I suppose. Tom didn't react. Instead, he turned to me and said, "Give me the rifle." For a second I hesitated, so he simply grabbed it from me. He could have done it at any point, I guess. And I guess he knew that, too. He raised the gun and pointed it at Travis's head.

"You will answer my questions, Travis. The first one you don't, I pull the trigger on this rifle and put another hole through your face."

"You got it, Captain," Travis snarled.

"You had any dreams lately? Any you can't explain?"

"I don't dream," he said. "Ain't never, ain't startin' now."

"How'd you know how to cook that rabbit?"

"Hell, Captain, it's meat. You put it in the pan and watch it burn. How hard can it be? But I damn sure wasn't gonna eat any of it."

Tom lowered the rifle and turned to me and Andy.

"He sounds right, and he sounds like himself."

"You can't know that, Tom," I said.

"Yeah, Captain," Andy added. "Was him was cursed. Was him the old woman wanted. I say we give him to her."

"I don't know," Tom said.

"Tell him, Jack," Andy begged. He was shaking, and I thought he might cry. He wasn't fit to take much more of this. "Tell him. You're the one who found Joe. You're the one who found him all emptied out, skin off of him like somebody was making him into a suit."

"It's true, Tom," I said, but even in the saying it, something wasn't right.

Tom creased his brow.

"I suppose," Tom said. He looked as if he had made a decision. But now I wasn't thinking about Travis anymore.

"Wait," I almost whispered. "Andy, that about Joe, how'd you know that?"

Tom and Andy both looked at me funny. "What are you talking about, Jack?" Tom asked.

"How'd he know that? I didn't tell him. You told me not to."

Tom still looked at me like I was crazy. But then his eyes showed some recognition. "Yeah," Tom said, his mind starting to clear, "yeah, I did. How did you know that, Andy?"

"I don't know," Andy said. "What's this all about?"

"I only told Doc Stanley, and I was the last person to talk to him," I said. "Come on, Andy, how'd you know that?"

"Well," Andy stammered, looking pale and thin, like he was scared to death, "I just…just…" And then his voice changed. "Oh

Hell," he growled. He grinned, wider than I thought a man's face should go. Then he started to laugh. As his laugh grew deeper and louder, his face began to split. Where his smile should have met his cheek, the skin began to crack, like a man had taken a knife and sliced him from the corner of his mouth to his ear. I fell back in sheer terror. His head was literally flapping back and forth on his laugh, and his eyes had grown as red as fire. Tom fell back beside me, but to his credit, he raised his rifle and fired it at Andy's heart. Andy stopped laughing. He cocked his head sharply to the right, and then he let loose an open-mouthed howl, a roar from some ancient, horrible world that shook me to my core.

No shame in saying it, I turned and ran, and Tom was running right beside me. We ran until the howl was only an echo, until we were deep in the forest. If I hadn't tripped on a root and fallen, with Tom stumbling over me, we might still be running today.

We lay there like that, not wanting to move, not wanting to believe what had happened. All around us still echoed the now distant howl, the roar I suspect few men on this Earth have lived to describe. The night was thick and dark. Only the pale, now waning, moon provided any light. The trees shook though there was no wind, and just beyond my sight seemed to move creatures and phantasms from another world, one long past if it ever really was. Finally, I spoke.

"God, Tom, what do we do?"

"We run, Jack. We run, and we don't look back."

We sat there while I thought about what he had said. He was right, of course. But at the same moment I made that decision, a scream came ringing through the forest—it was Travis's voice, though not in any form I had ever heard before. I looked at Tom, and he looked at me. I had no love for Travis, and neither did Tom. But that scream. I knew at that moment that it would be a mortal sin to leave him behind. It was death or damnation now, that was all there was. Tom exhaled deeply. He had come to the same conclusion.

"We go back, then," Tom said. "But I don't know what we do when we get there. I hit him right in the chest, right in the chest at point blank range, and it didn't faze him. Didn't even slow him down."

"There's a mirror in my tent," I said, "that I use for shaving. It's small, but it might work."

Tom's eyes brightened. There was no need to explain. As I have come to learn, the men of the woods all know the legend of the Wendigo in full.

We made our way back to the campsite. Even in the dark, it wasn't hard to find our way. Travis's ever-loudening screams served as the perfect map. When we reached the edge of the woods along the clearing where our camp was set up, a horrible sight met our eyes. Only the fire still burned where we had left it. Our things were strewn about the ground. The two horses were dead, whether from an attack or fright, I couldn't tell. But it was Travis I will never forget. He was still tied to the wagon wheel and still alive, though barely. His stomach was sliced open, and his bowels spilled out onto the ground. Andy, or the thing that had been Andy, was on its hands and knees, shoveling Travis's intestines into its mouth. That Travis was still conscious made it all the worse. I looked over to where my tent once stood. It had collapsed, and I couldn't be sure that anything was where I had left it. Given Travis's state, it was surely an empty gesture anyway.

"Well?" Tom asked.

"I don't know, Tom. Travis is dead. His body just hasn't caught up to the fact. Maybe you were right before. Maybe we should just go."

I saw Tom purse his lips in thought.

"Naw," he finally said, making a decision. "Naw, I was wrong before. We can't run. He'd track us down. No doubt about that. Even if he couldn't before, Joe was the best tracker I ever met. And he has his talents now. No, we got only one choice, and that is to stop him here. You think you can still get that mirror?"

I looked back at my wrecked tent. I couldn't be sure.

"I can try, Tom, but I can't promise it."

"Well, then," Tom said firmly, "that'll have to do. Let's get down there. If he doesn't notice you, all the better. If he does, I'll distract him as best I can. You get that mirror, and do what needs to be done."

I nodded. Tom held out his hand. I grabbed it, and he shook firmly. And then reluctantly but quickly, we made our way down the hill and into the camp.

* * *

We stopped at the edge, and Tom motioned for me to go on. He would remain in the shadows. If we were lucky, he would stay there. I stole quietly across the grounds, taking cover behind a lonely tree whenever I could. But it didn't take long till there was nothing but open ground between me and my tent. It was still ten yards off. Not a long distance on most days, but an eternity with a beast like the Wendigo in your sights.

I sat there for a good minute, watching him. He was oblivious to me, his hands working a string of Travis's intestines like it was a line of sausage. Travis wasn't screaming anymore. He just moaned. I doubt if he was in his right mind. I thought about what I would do, what was the best I could hope for. That thought sent a chill to my bones. Even if I found the mirror, it would mean confronting that thing. And if it didn't work, death, and probably not a quick one, was assured.

Now I could wait no longer, I took a deep breath and moved toward my tent as fast as possible while still staying silent. It was no easy task. Seven yards away. There were pots and pans, traps, boxes, and everything you could imagine you might need on that kind of trip, strewn about all over the ground. I dodged them as best I could. If he heard me then…well, I didn't want to think on it.

Now I was five yards from the tent. I looked back at the Wendigo. He was still hunched over, still consuming his meal. Three yards. What was left of another tent had been thrown clear across the field and lay in between me and my destination. I walked around, but it just meant more time I was in the open.

Finally, I reached the remains of my tent. But the ordeal wasn't over. I crouched at the side where my shaving kit should be. I sat there, for God and all his angels to see, feeling blindly under the canvas, trying not to make a sound while also looking with my hands for a small object I didn't even know was there.

I could hear the sickening sound of the beast, not more than fifty feet beyond, his teeth ripping through flesh. I looked over at him. Still he continued to feed. The sound of his mouth working bloody meat grew louder and louder till I thought it would steal my mind. On I worked, feeling about, trying to find the one thing that might save me. That noise continued, like a drumbeat in my brain. Then, finally, blessedly, it stopped. I said a quick prayer of thanks and searched on with new vigor.

But then I felt cold fear fall over me. I looked over at the Wendigo. There it sat, blood and muscle hanging from its mouth and hands, its demon red eyes locked on me. I froze, but the low growl that started deep in the pit of its flesh-gorged stomach spurned me into feverish action. I made no attempt to be quiet now, feeling desperately for my mirror.

The roar grew louder until finally it burst from what had been Andy's mouth in a hellish, deafening sound. It loped toward me, running like some primordial beast, pushing with its legs and thrusting with its knuckles off the ground in great bounding leaps. All the while it screamed at me in a voice no human mouth ever made. It was upon me, and I knew it was the end.

Then there was a flash in the corner of my vision, and the beast, in mid-spring, was thrust to the side. It let out an almost pitiful yelp, like a dog kicked in the gut by an angry master. I sat there frozen, staring at the ax blade protruding from the side of Andy's contorted and barely recognizable face. I looked to the side to see Tom standing next to the fire, a flaming log in one hand and another ax in the other.

"Don't just sit there, kid! Find it!" he yelled.

I jerked back into action, feeling madly for the mirror. The Wendigo lay still for a moment, but then it began to push itself up. I began to give up hope. What if I had moved it? What if it were somewhere else in the wrecked camp? Panic set in. My vision became blurry. Tom's cries as the Wendigo righted itself and ripped the ax from its head began to seem more and more distant. It was as if I was falling into a deep well, far from the world around me.

I was shocked back to reality by a sharp pain that shot through my hand. In any other situation, I would have jerked it out, and all hope might have been lost. But I was so close to being gone that I just sat there, wondering what it could mean. Then it struck me—my razor! I had cut my hand, and that meant the mirror was close.

The Wendigo was up now, advancing on Tom. He held his ground, swinging the flaming log, but he couldn't hold the beast long. Then, salvation. My hand felt smooth, polished glass and the cold kiss of metal. I grabbed the mirror and pulled it out. I leapt to my feet, running toward the spot where the man and the beast were circling each other. But I was too late. With a brutal strike, the Wendigo, avoiding the torch, ripped open Tom's leg with a quick slice of his claws. Tom fell to the ground with a cry. The Wendigo poised itself over him, ready to make the killing blow. But at that moment, I jumped on his back, thrusting the mirror in his face.

I felt the demon shudder beneath me. Then, it let out a cry unlike the ones before, for this was a howl of pain. I fell backward off of him, and he fell to his knees, hands clasping his face. Tom, despite his injury, looked at me with a face beaming in triumph. But then, from where the Wendigo lay, came an unexpected sound. He was laughing.

It was a guttural laugh, a courage-stealing, soul-crushing laugh. It was a laugh that seemed to come from Andy's broken body and all around at the same time. It was a cruel, cold laugh, a rumbling, rolling laugh. The Wendigo lifted itself from the ground. It turned around, not even noticing Tom lying not more than a few feet from him. It turned and glared at me, and Andy's split face seemed to smile.

"Pitiful child," it said, in a voice that was not Andy's, one I seemed to hear in my mind rather than in my ears. "Superstitions and petty tricks do not harm me."

I stumbled backward, nearly falling over a burning log. I stooped down and picked it up, swinging it wildly at the loping beast before me. It laughed again.

"I do not fear fire or flame, the gift of my race to your primitive fathers. We, who walked among the stars and will again. The ancients are not dead. No, they sleep only, but the time is coming of their waking. What is your life against ours? A blink, a whisper in the night, a flash that fades into darkness. So, do not fear your death. You will serve a grander purpose."

I continued to fall back, but he matched me step for step.

"Do not run. Your pain will feed me, your flesh will be my sustenance, and in your death, I will live. What is your end? Will you feed the worm? Or a god?"

It hit me then. I would not survive. I could not run. There was simply nowhere to go. I stopped backing up. If he was to take me, I would face him. He took another step toward me and another. And, then, I felt myself transported back, back to something my father once told me. I was a young boy of twelve. My father had taken me aside.

"Jack," he said, "this is dangerous business, and a man who lives by the forest may well die by it."

My father was not an educated man. I guess he never had any schooling at all. But he was wise, wise in a way that a man only gets through hard experience. He knew one bit of Latin I suppose. Just one bit. And he taught me it that day.

"Always remember this, Jack. If the breaks go against you, if you are staring death in the face, *in hoc signo vinces*. In this sign, you will conquer. Remember it, Jack, always. And if death comes, you'll die in His bosom."

The Wendigo was on me now, so close I could smell death on his breath. I looked down at the log next to me and accepted my fate. I took it, raised it in the air and brought it straight down. Then, I moved it from my left to right. In the darkness, the cross of flame I had cut into the night shimmered in front of me, though the flaming brandlog was now at my side. The Wendigo stopped, grinning at what I had done. He laughed.

"More foolish superstition?" he asked. "I wager this one will serve you no better."

Then, he took another step forward, his chest passing through the spot I had marked. I closed my eyes and prepared for death. But nothing happened. I ventured a look and saw the Wendigo standing in front of me, his blood red eyes peeled back, his mouth hanging open in what can only be described as shock. He took a step backward, and his knees began to shake. He grabbed at his heart.

"No!" he cried, in shock as much as pain. I stood there dumbfounded as flame burst from his chest. I watched as it spread, consuming the beast before my eyes. In haunted cries, he broke from one unknown language to another, speaking words whose meaning I do not wish to know.

The beast fell to his knees. But then, as the flames threatened to consume him, he looked at me and said, "The body dies, but the spirit lives on."

I saw his eyes change, saw the red drain from them. In the instant before he died, I saw the eyes of Andy. And though he was in unimaginable pain, they were filled with gratitude and joy.

I suppose that is the end of the story, though it was not the end of the ordeal. The horses were dead, and Tom could barely walk. I took a bear skin and made it so that I could pull it behind me. Tom lay inside, and I began to drag him through the snow, back through the forest to the town that lay miles beyond. We had no supplies, no provisions. But I was not concerned. I could trap something, find something. But as we moved on, it was as if every animal in the forest had vanished, as if we were truly cursed. There was no food then, nothing to eat, nothing to catch. A man can go a long time without food, but not in the cold, not when he is dragging another behind him. Things happen in times like that, things you try and forget, things you don't talk about. Five days later, Tom died. Seven days after that, I stumbled into the village. Alone, but not starved.

That was fifty years ago, fifty years in which I have made the forest my home. I never saw the Wendigo again, not in the flesh at least. But there were times when the night was dark and cold, when the moon was full in the sky and the icy wind would cut through flesh and bone. In those times, I would hear a voice on the wind and my dreams would be filled with flashes of light and peals of thunder, of dark shapes moving in the distance, and the screeching cry of a great bird seeking its prey.

Brett J. Talley is the Bram Stoker Award nominated author of That Which Should Not Be, The Void, and He Who Walks In Shadow. His work has been featured in the shared-world anthology, Limbus, Inc., and he is the editor of Limbus, Inc. Vols. II & III. He is also a lawyer, speechwriter, and an avid fan of the Alabama Crimson Tide. He makes his internet home on his website, www.brettjtalley.com.

HE WHO
WALKS IN
SHADOW

BRETT J. TALLEY

BRETT J. TALLEY

THAT
WHICH
SHOULD
NOT BE

www.ingramcontent.com/pod-product-compliance
Lightning Source LLC
Chambersburg PA
CBHW021009180626
46814CB00003B/1214